Beckett Blaise

That Bastard The Vampire

Rose and Raven Vampire Surveys Book I

AF094940

Shadesilver Publishing

Join in on the fun!

My newsletter has free books, sales on books, exclusive deals, and more. You can also get the latest news on my new releases! Just scan the QR code below.

That Bastard the Vampire

Copyright © 2025 by Beckett Blaise

All rights reserved.

No part of this book may be reproduced in any form or by any electronic or mechanical means, including information storage and retrieval systems, without written permission from the author, except for the use of brief quotations in a book review.

This is a work of fiction. Names, characters, businesses, places, events, and incidents are either the product of the author's imagination or are used fictitiously. Any resemblance to actual persons, living or dead, events, or locals is entirely coincidental

Contact info: cleavebourbon@gmail.com

Front Cover Design by Shadesilver Publishing.

Print Cover Design by Shadesilver Publishing.

Editor: Mark E. Tyson

FIRST EDITION : APRIL 2025

10 9 8 7 6 5 4 3 2 1

Beckett Blaise

That Bastard the Vampire

——•────◆⟨∞⟩◆────•——

Rose and Raven Vampire Surveys Book I

Shadesilver Publishing

CONTENTS

Prologue: Prey		1
1.	Chapter 1: Seth Aubrey	4
2.	Chapter 2: Something Out of Sync	11
3.	Chapter 3: First Meeting	19
4.	Chapter 4: Deeds and Doubts	28
5.	Chapter 5: Emily Laurence	37
6.	Chapter 6: An Ill-Conceived Decision	46
7.	Chapter 7: The Next Step	54
8.	Chapter 8: Fear and Truth	64
9.	Chapter 9: Small Victories	76
10.	Chapter 10: The Dark Purpose of Evil	85
11.	Chapter 11: Stranglehold	95
12.	Chapter 12: Time to Think	104
13.	Chapter 13: Ancient Knowledge	110
14.	Chapter 14: Making Plans, Making Moves	128
15.	Chapter 15: Of Words and Blood	137

16.	Chapter 16: The Fortress by the Sea	147
17.	Chapter 17: Betrayal and Redemption	157
18.	Chapter 18: Between Worlds	168
19.	Chapter 19: The Seventh Manuscript	178
20.	Chapter 20: Shadow of the Eclipse	187
21.	Chapter 21: No More Sacrifices	196
22.	Chapter 22: Broken Dreams of Immortality	205
23.	Chapter 23: Confined to Shadow	213
24.	Chapter 24: The Path of the Chronicler	223
25.	Chapter 25: The First Book	233
26.	Chapter 26: That Bastard the Vampire	243
Epilogue: Future Landscapes		253
About the author		257

Prologue
Prey

Fog rolled through the cobblestone streets of London, wrapping around Margaret's ankles as she fled past darkened shop windows. Her boots clicked against the stones, each step echoing off brick walls that seemed to close in around her. The gaslights cast weak circles of yellow through the murk, barely penetrating the darkness between them.

Something followed. Not the clip-clop of hooves or the shuffle of a cutpurse. This presence moved like silk over stone, soundless yet impossible to ignore. Margaret's heart hammered against her ribs. She darted down an alley, her skirts tangling around her legs.

"Keep running, keep running," she whispered, but her feet slowed of their own accord. The fog thickened, and with it came a scent of leather and spice and something metallic that made her mouth water.

Her fingers trembled as she braced against a wall. The rough brick scraped her palms. She should scream. Should cry for help. But her throat had gone dry, and in place of terror, a strange warmth spread through her limbs.

"Lost, my dear?" The voice drifted from the shadows, smooth as aged brandy.

Margaret spun around. The alley stretched empty behind her, yet she could feel eyes upon her skin. "Who's there?"

A chuckle floated on the night air. "Someone who could help you find your way."

"I know my way." But she didn't move. Couldn't move. Her legs had turned to lead, even as her mind screamed at her to flee.

"Do you? Then why are you here, in this dark place, at this dark hour?" The voice drew closer, wrapping around her like smoke.

"I was..." Margaret frowned. Why had she come this way? She remembered leaving the millinery shop, taking her usual route home, but then... nothing. Just the overwhelming urge to turn down these twisted streets.

"You came because I called." A figure materialized from the fog ahead. Tall, elegant, with a face that belonged in a classical painting. He stepped into the weak lamplight, and Margaret's breath caught.

Dark hair fell in waves past his collar. His evening clothes were immaculate, a black tailcoat and waistcoat that emphasized his broad shoulders. But it was his eyes that held her. They gleamed like polished amber in the gaslight, ancient and hungry.

"Sebastian Wolfram." He bowed, never breaking eye contact. "At your service."

Margaret's hand flew to her throat. "I should go."

"Should you?" Sebastian glided closer. Each step was liquid grace, a predator's dance. "Or perhaps this is exactly where you're meant to be."

Her back pressed against the wall. The brick was cold through her dress, but her skin burned wherever his gaze touched. "Please..."

"Shhh." He reached out, one gloved finger trailing along her jaw. "Don't fight it, my dear. You've been looking for me all your life, haven't you? Something missing, something you could never quite name?"

She had. God help her, she had. Every novel that failed to satisfy, every suitor who seemed pale and lifeless in comparison to her dreams. She'd been searching for this, for him.

Sebastian's smile revealed teeth too sharp to be natural. "There now. No more running."

His hand cupped the back of her neck, and Margaret melted into his embrace. The last thing she saw were those amber eyes, burning with ancient hunger as his lips descended toward her throat.

Chapter 1
Seth Aubrey

Seth clicked on his voice recorder. "I probably should begin this dictation with an introduction. My name is Seth Byron Aubrey. I am a writer. No, scratch that, rewind. Okay, 3, 2...I should begin by introducing myself. My name is Seth Byron Aubrey. I am a researcher and biographer. I have written several biographies of important men and women who have made an impact in our world. I have even written a few about people who currently impact our world. Oh, that's terrible. God, I sound so self-important. Screw it. I'm just going to go with it and edit it out later." He cleared his throat. "All right, in 3, 2... I am about to enter the Rose and Raven Society's headquarters in their very secret location. They want to interview me on the materials I have gathered on Sabastian Elijah Wolfram over the past two years, but before I go in, I wanted to commit a few things to this recording in the unlikely case something should happen to me. Sabastian, he sometimes likes to go by the name Wolf from his surname, originally hired me to write his official biography. Usually, I write about people's lives long after they have died, and this one is no exception. Sabastian Wolfram, Wolf, is indeed dead, just not in the conventional sense. He's a vampire.

Recently, I have come to understand just how villainous vampires can be. I bought into the notion that they were charming and sophisticated just like every other poor slob who has seen a recent Hollywood vampire flick, but they are neither charming nor sophisticated. It's all an act. They are in fact vicious, dangerous predators and assholes. In a few moments, I am going to walk into the Rose and Raven Society and give them all the information they desire so they can hunt the bastard down and in a perfect world kill him. I took his money to write a biography, and I'm going to follow through with it, only it's not the sugarcoated shit he wanted me to write. No, I am going to write his biography all right, his unauthorized biography!" He looked up when the front door of the building opened and a nice-looking woman wearing a blue dress exited. "Okay, here we go. They are coming out to get me. If anyone should find this recording and not find me, go to Connie Stone at 411 Second Street. Tell her you want the spaghetti with garlic sauce. She will know what to do."

"Are you ready, Seth?" The woman asked.

"I am." He put his recorder away.

"Follow me, then."

He followed her through the doorway into the antique hallways of the old, yet opulent, society headquarters. The place seemed to be completely adorned with ancient, polished wood. The woman led him to a room with two lush chairs facing each other and a small table with two bottles of water placed on it. A camara and its operator were off to the right of the chairs ready to record their conversation.

"Right here, Seth. May I get you anything?"

Seth sat in the indicated chair. "No, I see you have a water for me. That's all I need."

She smiled and left.

He looked at his mobile phone to make sure it was on silent and to check it. No one had called him since yesterday. He put it away and returned to his voice recorder. He could do that same recording on his phone, but he didn't trust having everything on one device. He clicked the record button, "I am about to be interviewed. They are going to record it for their own records. While the cameraman sets up, I wanted to add one more thing to the narrative. I'm sure Emily is Wolf's vampire consort by now. I hope they stake her through the heart too!"

Seth straightened up when he saw the pretty blonde interviewer enter the room. She sat in the opposite chair and an assistant rushed over to place her microphone and ear plug. Once it was in place she smiled. "Seth is it?"

"Yes, ma'am."

"My name is Ann Franklin. I'll be interviewing you today." She held out her hand.

"Pleased to meet you, Ann." He took her hand, and she gave him a dainty, weak handshake then pulled her hand away rather quickly.

"Okay, Seth, just speak to me like we're having a normal everyday conversation."

"That's easy for you to say, Ann, you're used to this kind of thing." Seth checked his hair again. "Is my hair still okay?"

"Gorgeous, I wish my natural color was as dark and luxurious as yours with no grey. How do you not have grey at your age."

"Oh, there's grey. I pluck those babies out!"

"I wouldn't have any hair left if I did that. I have to dye mine."

"You mean you are not a true blue eyed blonde? Shocking."

"Hey, I complimented you!"

"Sorry, force of habit. I tend to rattle off at the mouth when I'm nervous."

"Let's start right there. What do you have to be nervous about?"

"Easy, I am nervous about that bastard the vampire. He has eyes and ears everywhere. He is vindictive too. He might even have people here in the Rose and Raven Building."

She chuckled. "I want you to know that's highly unlikely. Are you afraid he is going to burst in here or something? I assure you. If he did have anyone here, they would be found out rather quickly."

She was so calm and natural that he didn't know if this was part of the interview or idle conversation. "Oh, are you interviewing me now?"

"The society has eyes and ears everywhere too, and I assure you this is a safe place. You are safe from him. Why don't you start from the beginning?"

He looked at the camera. There was a blinking red light, "Are we recording?"

She peered over at the camera operator, and he nodded. "Yes, we're recording."

"And I can get a copy of this? I haven't written this stuff down yet and that recording might come in handy. I have always been great at telling stories and I might just be able to write it down word for word."

"Yes, you will get a copy."

"Okay, first of all, Wolf is not a particularly old vampire. He was born in 1919 in San Antonio, Texas. He was twenty-two when the japs bombed Pearl Harbor so, he, like most men his age, signed up for the service. By all accounts, he was a normal, red blooded American kid looking to make a life for himself. World War II in Europe, that's where it all changed for him. That's where he became a vampire."

"You shouldn't say japs, Seth."

"Why? That's what they are."

"This is the twenty first century, Seth."

"All right, he was fighting enemies in World War II."

"He was in the army?"

"Well, yes, he was. Which regiment or division I have no idea. He changes the story often. Sometimes he stormed the beaches on D-Day, sometimes he parachuted in with the 101st Airborne, and sometimes he is British.

"So, you don't know for certain?"

"No, his service records were conveniently destroyed in a fire with many of the other soldiers' records. I did meet with one soldier who said he served with him in the 101st Airborne, but at the time of my interview with him, he was ninety-seven and his memory was not good, but it's the best information I have."

He opened the bottle of water and took a sip, "Okay, let's get to it. Vampires love wartime. They can run around battlefields and feed almost to their evil hearts' content. Many of them become medics. They can easily take a drink from the unconscious wounded while they are bandaging them up. Being a medic also means they are supposed to be left alone by the enemy while treating wounded, although that doesn't always happen. Sometimes the enemy fires on the medics, which is a mistake if that medic is a vampire."

"Can they be killed on the battlefield?"

"Yes and no. They have to be careful. They can regenerate an arm or leg but if they get blown into pieces, that's harder to recover from, but they can even do that. That's what happened to the vampire who turned him. According to his account the vamp had an arm blown off and she was missing a leg. She happened to crawl up on his fox hole when he was alone. He damn near took her head off but she charmed him. She was wounded so she almost bled him dry but for whatever reason, she had a moment of remorse, or she had a moment of clarity and cruelty, because she opened up a vein on her arm and drained some of the blood back into Wolf's mouth. That is the act that turned him."

"What was a woman doing out in battle in World War II?"

"Like I said, if she could get around unseen, a battlefield is a perfect buffet for vamps. She doesn't have to go through the whole death and murder scene to get human blood. I don't know why she was out there. I always assumed it was as Wolf told it and she was out feeding when she got too close to the action and got herself wounded."

"Okay, let's focus on that for a moment. A female vampire was roaming an active battlefield looking for blood. That does sound far-fetched. What would you say to those who do not believe in vampires?

"I say every culture on this damn planet has a legend of a blood sucking humanoid parasite. Man has lived in fear of them for centuries. They can blend into human society and walk among us. Only the greedy, stupid ones get caught because their need for blood sometimes presents as something like an addiction. Those vampires who can control their intense hunger are the dangerous ones. Wolf is one of those. I get the feeling sometimes he doesn't need the blood as bad as other vampires, like he get sustenance from another source too."

"Now, that's interesting. What other source could he feed from, food?"

"No, not food. It's hard to explain. He just doesn't seem to have the blood lust as bad as regular vamps. He is satiated longer, or he feeds on something in addition to blood, which one it is I have no idea." He looked her in the eye, "You say you don't believe in vampires? If you don't, then you are their perfect victim. You had better watch your back in the still of the darkest night because they are out there, Ann, and they are hunting you."

Chapter 2
Something Out of Sync

Seth examined the envelope in his hand carefully. It was made of heavy paper and sealed tightly with wax. His name gleamed in perfect copper-plate calligraphy across the front. No return address. Just his name and apartment number in Manhattan's less fashionable eastern blocks.

The letter opener sliced clean through the wax seal. It was an ornate 'W' pressed into dark red wax that looked almost black in the dim light of his study. Inside, the invitation card matched the envelope's quality, edges gilt in gold leaf.

"The pleasure of your company is requested..." Seth read aloud, squinting at the almost unreadable flowing script. "Thursday evening, 8 PM sharp. 180 Riverside Drive, Penthouse."

Penthouse! Riverside Drive meant old money and serious connections. The kind of break he'd been chasing for years. But something about the invitation nagged at him. The paper felt cool to touch, like it had been stored in a cellar. And that wax seal... in this century, who still sealed letters with wax?

A shadow passed across his window. Seth jerked his head up, catching a glimpse of... something. A figure, maybe? But his apartment was four stories up. It must have been a bird.

He turned back to the invitation. The date was off. The invitation specified Thursday the 13th, but when he checked his phone calendar, this Thursday was actually the 12th.

"Whatever," he muttered, tossing the invitation onto his desk. Rich people could afford their eccentricities, and this could be exactly what he needed. A wealthy patron interested in his work, someone to fund his next biography, was more than he could hope for. No more scraping by writing hit pieces and tabloid exposés.

The sun had set while he examined the invitation, leaving his study in shadow. Seth reached for the lamp switch but paused. Across the street, a man stood perfectly still in the window directly opposite his in the gathering dark. He was just visible in the fading twilight. He was tall, elegant in what looked like an expensive suit. He couldn't be sure in the low light. Their eyes felt like they met for just a moment. The stranger's smile was brilliant, predatory. Then Seth blinked and the man was gone.

A chill ran down his spine. He switched on every light in the apartment but couldn't shake the feeling of being watched. The invitation seemed to mock him from his desk, that dark red seal catching the light like a drop of blood.

His phone buzzed. He checked it to see a text from his girlfriend, Faith, asking about dinner plans. Seth grabbed his jacket, eager to get out of the suddenly oppressive apartment. As he reached for the invitation to tuck it into his pocket, he noticed something odd. The paper had grown even colder, and the gilt edges seemed to have darkened, as if tarnished by time.

He dismissed it as odd and went on his way. He was being too observant, too critical. Who cares what the invitation is made of; the potential payoff was too good to pass up. Seth slipped the invitation into his jacket and headed for the door, deliberately ignoring the way the shadows in the corners of his apartment seemed deeper than usual, how they seemed to shift and writhe when viewed from the corner of his eye. It was all in his overactive imagination. Just like when he was a kid taking out the garbage at nightfall. He let the darkness of the alley get to him, imagining some monster lurking there. He would toss the trash and then sprint back to the house as if someone were chasing him every time. The shadows in his apartment now were no different. There was nothing within them!

He set his mind back to the invitation and the money a new biography could bring. He'd dealt with plenty of wealthy eccentrics in his career. This was just another job, another chance at the success that had eluded him. Still, as he locked his apartment door, Seth couldn't shake the feeling that by accepting this invitation, he was stepping into something far bigger and darker than he realized.

The elevator dinged and he stepped inside, checking the invitation one final time. In the fluorescent light, he could have sworn the elegant script had changed, the letters somehow more angular and ancient. But when he blinked, it looked normal again. He'd seen shifting ink before. Two layers of ink where only became viewable at one angle or light source and one became viewable at a different angle or under a different light source. It was a neat effect.

Seth pushed through the revolving doors of Angelina's, the Italian restaurant's warm air and delectable smells hitting him like a wall after the autumn chill outside. The maître d' led him to their usual corner table where Faith already waited, her dark curls cascading over one shoulder as she studied the menu.

"You're late." She didn't look up, but a smile played at the corners of her mouth.

"Got caught up with something interesting." Seth slid into his seat, "A potential new client."

"Another exposé?" Faith set down her menu, fixing him with those piercing brown eyes. "I thought you were done with those."

"This is different." He pulled out the invitation, hesitating before placing it on the white tablecloth. The paper seemed to absorb the warm candlelight rather than reflect it. "Look at this."

Faith picked it up, her perfectly manicured nails tracing the seal. Her expression shifted from curiosity to concern. "This paper... it's old. Really old. And cold?" She set it down like it might bite. "Who sent it?"

"That's the interesting part." Seth leaned forward, lowering his voice. "No sender listed. Just an address on Riverside Drive."

"Riverside! The rich part of town?" Faith's eyebrows shot up. "Since when do *your* subjects live there?"

"They don't. That's why."

A shadow fell across their table. Seth looked up to find their waiter standing impossibly still, pen poised over his notepad. Had he been there the whole time? The man's face stayed fixed in a pleasant smile that didn't reach his eyes.

"Are you ready to order?" The waiter's voice carried an accent Seth couldn't place.

"Give us a minute." Faith waved him off, but the waiter's gaze lingered on Seth for a beat too long before he glided away. "That was weird."

Seth rubbed his arms, trying to shake off a sudden chill. "Everything's weird today. First that guy in the window opposite my apartment."

"What guy?"

"Nobody. Just..." Seth trailed off as he spotted someone through the restaurant's front window. The same tall figure from earlier stood across the street, motionless amid the flowing crowd of pedestrians. As Seth watched, the stranger raised a hand in greeting, then vanished behind a passing bus.

"Seth?" Faith touched his hand. "You're white as a sheet."

He jerked his attention back to her. "Sorry, thought I saw..." The words died in his throat as he noticed the invitation had changed position on the table, now aligned perfectly with the edge, the seal facing up. Neither of them had touched it.

"Maybe we should skip dinner." Faith's voice carried an edge of worry. "You don't look well."

"No, I'm fine." Seth forced a laugh that sounded hollow even to his ears. "Just letting my imagination run wild. You know how I get with new projects."

But as their waiter approached again, Seth noticed the man's movements were too smooth, his shadow too dark against the wall. And was it his imagination, or did those perfectly white teeth come to slightly sharper points than they should?

Seth reached for his water glass, his hand trembling slightly. The liquid inside had frozen solid.

Faith gasped. "Seth, the invitation-"

He looked down. The elegant script had definitely changed, the letters now twisted into ancient symbols that hurt his eyes to look at. But they shifted back to normal English even as he watched, leaving him wondering if he'd imagined it.

"Let's get out of here." Seth grabbed the invitation, shoving it deep into his pocket. The paper felt like a shard of ice against his leg.

As they stood to leave, he caught their waiter watching from across the room, that fixed smile still in place. The man raised his hand in an echo of the stranger's gesture from the street, and Seth could have sworn his eyes flashed red in the candlelight.

Seth burst through Angelina's doors, dragging Faith by the hand into the crisp night air. The invitation, cold in his pocket, gave him the creeps, but he couldn't bring himself to throw it away. "It still meant money and the possibility of prestige with a wealthy client.

"What's going on?" Faith pulled back, her heels clicking on the sidewalk. "Talk to me."

"I don't know." Seth scanned the crowded street. No sign of the tall stranger. "Something's not right. The invitation, that waiter, the man across the street."

"What man? I didn't see anyone."

A taxi blared its horn as it sped past, making Seth jump. The city felt different somehow. In his paranoia it had become darker, more hostile. Even the familiar neon signs of his neighborhood seemed to cast strange, unrecognizable glows.

"Come back to my place." Faith squeezed his arm. "You're obviously exhausted. When's the last time you slept properly?"

Seth reached into his pocket. The envelope still would not warn up, not even from his body heat. "I need to figure this out. That address on Riverside Drive."

"Can wait until tomorrow." Faith stepped into the street, waving down a cab. "Whatever this is, you're in no state to-"

The streetlight above them flickered and died. In the sudden darkness, Seth caught a whiff of something ancient, like the inside of an old library, or inside a dusty crypt. He caught a whiff of roses too. When the light sputtered back on, their waiter from Angelina's stood on the corner, still holding his notepad. His smile remained fixed, mechanical.

"Your bill, sir." The waiter extended his arm. The notepad's pages fluttered in the wind.

"We didn't order anything." Seth backed away, pulling Faith with him.

"Nevertheless." The waiter's smile widened, revealing teeth that definitely came to points. "Payment is due."

A cab screeched to a halt beside them. Seth yanked open the door, practically shoving Faith inside. As he dove in after her, he looked for the waiter's reflection in the window, but there wasn't one. The man cast no shadow at all.

"East 82nd Street," Faith told the driver, her voice shaking. "And hurry."

Seth turned to look out the rear window. The waiter had vanished, but a tall figure in an expensive suit stood beneath the next streetlight, raising one hand in that same deliberate greeting.

"What's happening to me?" He slumped against the seat.

Faith took his hand. Her warmth helped drive back the chill that had settled into his bones. "We'll figure it out. But first, you need rest."

The cab wound through Manhattan's crowded streets. Seth tried to focus on Faith's hand in his, on the familiar rhythm of the city at night. It made him feel better.

"Thursday the 13th," he muttered, thinking about the impossible date. "Tomorrow night."

"Don't even think about it." Faith's grip on his hand tightened. "Whatever this is, it might not be worth the time, money or effort. After tonight, perhaps you should abandon the idea."

Seth shook his head, "No, I will at least see what this person has to offer. It could set us up for life. We could finally get that bigger apartment and move in together."

"That would be wonderful. All right, I will leave it up to your judgement."

The cab's radio sprang to life, spitting static and fragments of what sounded like Latin chanting. Their driver cursed, reaching for the dial. He glimpsed them from the rearview mirror, "Sorry about that folks. This radio has been busted for a week."

"It's okay," Seth said. "There's another ten spot in it if you step on it."

"Yes sir," The cabbie said as he pressed on the gas pedal.

Chapter 3
First Meeting

Seth marveled at the way the one percent lived as the elevator doors opened directly into the penthouse. Moonlight streamed through two skylights illuminating the room. In the dim light, he could see the marble floors and priceless artworks hanging in shadows. The space felt impossibly vast for Manhattan.

"Mr. Aubrey." A deep. smooth voice said from somewhere unseen. "Right on time."

Sebastian Wolfram emerged from behind a grand piano, his movements fluid and precise. His face bore the sharp angles of youth, but his eyes... Seth swallowed hard. Those eyes could see right through him.

"How did you-" Seth glanced back at the elevator. He hadn't pressed a button. Hadn't needed to.

"Get comfortable." Sebastian gestured to a leather armchair. The crystal tumbler beside it filled with amber liquid. "I have taken the liberty of pouring you a drink. We have much to discuss."

Seth moved to the chair and glanced at the aged whiskey. It smelled like his father's favorite brand, but that would be impossible since it was discontinued thirty years ago.

"Your reputation precedes you." Sebastian settled across from him. "The biographer who exposes secrets. The truth-teller."

"I try to be accurate." Seth's throat felt dry. Against his better judgment, he reached for the whiskey.

"Accuracy?" Sebastian laughed, the sound echoing in the cavernous apartment. "Tell me in your expert opinion. How old would you say I am?"

Seth studied his host's face. "Thirty-five, maybe forty?"

"The truth," Sebastian said, settling back into his chair, "is whatever the storyteller decides it to be."

"That's not strictly true." Seth said. "If I were to decide you were eighty-seven I doubt many people would believe me, especially if they see you or see a picture of you."

He hesitated, looking Seth uncomfortably in the eye, "I do not allow pictures to be taken of me. Should you pose my age to be eighty-seven that is what it would be to your readers unless they were able to see me and prove otherwise, which is unlikely since I do not mingle in social gatherings. I stick to the night in my outings. I find the city more peaceful when most people are sleeping instead of crowding the streets."

Seth's whiskey glass slipped from numb fingers. It should have shattered, but Sebastian caught it, moving from across the room at break-neck speed, and set it gently on the table.

"Impossible." Seth pressed back into his chair. "You're using projectors, or mirrors."

"Your skepticism is charming." Sebastian appeared suddenly beside him, breath cold against Seth's ear. "But we both know better."

Seth's adrenaline rose making his heart beat faster. The room spun. Everything he thought he knew about reality crumbled like ancient parchment.

"I want you to tell my story." Sebastian returned to his chair, or had he moved at all? "The true story. Not the tabloid versions, not the myths. My story, in my words."

"Why me?"

"Because you understand the power of truth. How it can be shaped, molded..." Sebastian smiled. "Your previous works demonstrate that perfectly."

Seth thought of his past biographies, and all the careers and reputations he'd destroyed with them simply by disclosing carefully chosen facts. His stomach churned. "You must know, I don't hold back, and I do not lie. I will expose your truth no matter what."

"Oh, I'm counting on it. You shall have what you need should you decide to write it for me. The advance alone would solve all your financial troubles." Sebastian produced a contract from the end table next to him. "And the story... well, it would make your career. Everything you've ever wanted."

He leaned forward and placed a pen into Seth's hand. Then he leaned back as he put the contract on the coffee table in front of him.

"All I need is your signature." Sebastian crossed one hand over the other as he sunk back into his plush chair. "Your word that you'll tell my truth."

Seth's hand trembled as he stared at the contract. He was never good at deciphering modern legalese. He blinked hard, but the words still had little meaning to him. "I need to show this to my lawyer before I sign."

"The terms are simple." Sebastian pulled an envelope from his jacket. "Five hundred thousand dollars. Just for signing. Another million upon completion."

Seth's breath caught. That kind of money *would* clear his debts and set him up for years. Hell, he could finally propose to Faith properly and give her the life she deserved.

"And what's the catch?" The words scraped his dry throat. "What's written in here that I should know about?"

"You mean the fine print?" Sebastian's laugh sounded a touch unnatural. "There is no catch, I assure you. Only that you tell the story as I direct. No unauthorized research. No digging into records or interviewing others. Just you and me, crafting the narrative I choose to share."

Seth's journalist instincts flared. "Ah, there it is. You see, I don't work like that. What you are proposing is not a biography. I am afraid that what you propose is the opposite of truth. In fact, it's propaganda."

"Is it?" Sebastian appeared beside the window, Manhattan's lights creating a halo around his silhouette. "Your last book, you know, the one about Senator Morrison. Did you include his charity work? His dedication to literacy programs?"

Heat crept up Seth's neck. "Those weren't relevant to-"

"To the story you wanted to tell." Sebastian's eyes flashed. "You chose which truths to highlight. Which to bury. We're not so different."

He was right, he did cherry pick the facts hoping to entice readers and to sell books. The contract beckoned. Seth thought of his empty bank account, of Faith's patient smile when he'd postponed their vacation again. Of the pitying looks from his agent.

Seth gripped the fountain pen Sabastian has given him and twirled it between his fingers. "Say I sign, what would you have me write?"

"I've lived a thousand lifetimes, Mr. Aubrey. Witnessed the rise and fall of empires. Loved, lost, killed, saved. I'm offering you the story of centuries." his voice grew louder, more firm, "the story of a lifetime."

"Under your control." Seth's fingers closed around the pen.

"Under my truth." Sebastian placed the advance envelope on the table. "You've built your career exposing the darkness in others. Now I'm offering you the chance to explore something greater. To tell a story that will echo through generations. Sign, Mr. Aubrey. Let me show you history through the eyes of one who lived it."

The pen hovered over the signature line. Seth thought of every compromise he'd made chasing stories, every half-truth he'd stretched into scandal. At least this time, the deception would be honest. He would find the truth and tell it the way he saw fit. Wolfram couldn't rob him of his integrity. He had done worse than written a guided biography. Besides, he could always do the research anyway and tell the story truthfully by using writer's discretion.

He signed.

Wolfram swooped down and took the contract as if Seth might change his mind and scratch out his signature.

Seth leaned back picking up the whiskey and taking a sip.

Wolfram's mouth curled into his unusual, toothy smile, "Welcome aboard." Sebastian extended his hand. His skin felt like winter marble against Seth's palm. "Shall we begin?"

Sebastian led him through the penthouse. The space seemed to stretch beyond what the building's footprint should allow, each room grander than the last. Oil paintings lined the walls. Their subjects' eyes following their progress down the corridor.

"Your collection is..." Seth squinted at a portrait that could have been a Rembrandt. The signature looked authentic.

"Original." Sebastian's lips curled. "I knew most of them personally."

Seth groped in his pocket for his notepad. He'd brought it out of habit but hadn't written a single word. How could he capture this? Who would believe him? He found his pen and got ready to take notes anyway. "Rembrandt died in 1609 in Amsterdam. You are claiming you knew him?"

"I said most of them. By now you must know what I am, who I am. I shouldn't have to say it."

"What? a creature of the night? I don't believe in such things."

"You will, my friend. To answer your question. I was born prior to World War II and that's when I...became who I am today."

"During World War II?"

"Yes."

They entered a study that belonged in a European castle. Floor-to-ceiling bookshelves stretched upward, laden with leather-bound volumes. Some titles gleamed with gold leaf, others were so ancient the spines had worn smooth.

"First editions?" Seth ran his finger along the spines, stopping at a familiar title. "This can't be-"

"Paradise Lost? John was rather proud of that one." Sebastian plucked the volume from the shelf. The pages fluttered as he opened it, revealing a handwritten inscription. "He had such vision for a mortal."

Seth's journalist instincts kicked in despite his fear. "Now you're claiming you knew Milton?"

"Claim?" Sebastian's laugh echoed off the books. "I inspired several passages. Though he took some creative liberties with my suggestions."

"Again with the seventeenth century. Milton died in like 1674. That was a bit before World War II"

"You have a remarkable grasp of dates."

"It's my job. You'll find I'm full of useless trivia. We biographers have to be so we can see through the embellishments and boasts of our subjects."

"Your skepticism is charming, but ultimately irrelevant." Sebastian set the book aside. "I chose you for your ability to shape narrative, not your belief in the supernatural." He sat in an armchair next to the bookshelf.

"Or in fairy tales." Seth said, joining him in a adjacent chair.

"If you see them as such, yes."

"Why now?" Seth gripped the armchair's edges. "Why tell your story after all this time?"

"The world is changing. Technology, social media, and camera phones are everywhere now. Soon, creatures like me will need to evolve or vanish into myth."

"Creatures like-" Seth coughed. "There are more?"

"Focus, Mr. Aubrey." Sebastian's eyes shined in the dim light. "My story first. The others can wait."

"I bought you this leather journal." He pointed to the book on the desk between them, its pages are blank and waiting for your pen. Seth reached for it, but Sebastian raised a hand. "Not yet. Tonight is for questions. For understanding the scope of what you've agreed to. You may take notes in your small notebook but let's leave the heavy writing until after we get to know each other a little better. Tell me, what do you know of the year 1462?"

"The Ottoman Empire was-" Seth started.

"Not the history books version." Sebastian leaned forward. "What do you know of the night Vlad Tepes lost his throne? I was there, you see. Though he never knew exactly what role I played in his downfall."

"Now you're saying you-"

"I'm saying, Mr. Aubrey, that your biography will need to cover quite a bit more ground than your usual works." Sebastian smiled, teeth glinting. "We have centuries to explore, after all. And only your lifetime to tell it in."

"What you're saying is this is going to be a tome of historical significance."

"If you do it justice and write it with conviction."

"When do we start?"

"We already have. The question is, are you prepared for what comes next?"

"Yes, I believe I am, Mr. Wolfram. Why don't you start at the beginning?" he readied himself to take notes.

Chapter 4
Deeds and Doubts

Seth stared at his laptop screen, comparing his interview notes with historical records. Something wasn't adding up. Sebastian's account of the 1462 Ottoman invasion contained details absent from any historical document - expected, given his claimed first-hand experience. But other elements contradicted established facts. For one, he claimed his life changed during World War II but immediately contradicted that information. Unless...he was not referring to himself becoming a vampire. Seth breathed in his frustration. "Well," he said to himself, "if he wanted to believe he was the tooth fairy, I would write that for a million-dollar payout."

Still, the man was not good at pretending. He didn't know enough about history. The dates he gave didn't match. Sebastian placed himself in Târgoviște during the infamous retreat, yet by another one of his accounts he suggested he'd been in Constantinople that same week. He was going to have to do some really creative writing to straighten it all out.

Seth rubbed his temples. The penthouse library stretched around him, Sebastian's collection of priceless artifacts gathering dust on mahogany shelves. Three weeks into the project, and the impossible had become almost routine. Almost.

A book slipped from his grasp, hitting the floor with a hollow thud. Seth bent to retrieve it, then paused. The sound wasn't right. He tapped his knuckles against the floorboards. The echo confirmed his suspicion. He had found an empty space beneath.

His fingers found the edge of a hidden panel. It lifted with surprising ease, revealing a compartment beneath. The smell hit him first, a mixture of musty leather and old paper. Dozens of journals filled the space, their covers worn with age.

"What's this now?" He pulled one out. The name embossed on the cover made his blood run cold: Richard C. Morrison, the true crime writer who'd vanished in '86. Seth had read his works, admired his unflinching style. The journal's final entry ended mid-sentence. The writer was the nephew of one of his own biography subjects, Senator Morrison. It was one hell of a coincidence.

Another journal belonged to Patricia Chen, the investigative reporter who'd "died in her sleep" in '92. More names he recognized. More unfinished stories.

His phone buzzed. An email notification from an anonymous account: "They all asked too many questions. Stop digging."

Attached was a PDF of a comprehensive list of writers and journalists who'd disappeared over the past century. Some names he knew. Others were new to him. All had been working on explosive stories before vanishing. He examined the text message again. It dawned on him that whoever sent it could see him. How else could the sender know what he was doing. He scanned the room seeing nothing unusual. He closed the floorboards and returned to his computer, not sure who had eyes on him.

Seth's fingers hovered over his keyboard. Two paths stretched before him. He could play it safe, stick to Sebastian's approved narrative. The advance alone would set him up for life. His girlfriend was already planning their dream wedding with the money.

Or he could dig deeper. Follow the trail of breadcrumbs these dead writers had left behind. Find the truth behind Sebastian's carefully constructed facade.

The library door creaked.

"Making progress?" Sebastian's voice drifted from the doorway.

"Just fact-checking some details." Seth closed his laptop, hoping his voice sounded steadier than his hands. "The Ottoman campaign is... complicated."

"History often is." Sebastian's footsteps echoed across the floor. "That's why perspective matters more than facts."

Seth thought of the dead writers' journals beneath his feet. Their unfinished investigations. Their silenced voices. He suppressed the urge to simply just ask him about them.

"What if..." Seth chose his words carefully. "What if I found a different perspective? One that didn't match your account?"

Sebastian's shadow fell across the desk as he neared. "Then I'd suggest you consider very carefully which version of the truth you wish to tell."

Seth's throat went dry as Sebastian circled the desk, each step deliberate and measured. The hidden compartment beneath his feet felt like a ticking bomb. One wrong move, one misplaced word, and everything would unravel.

"Your previous biographies were quite... scathing. The tech mogul expose was particularly brutal. Did you enjoy dismantling his legacy?"

"I followed the evidence." Seth said. "I followed the truth."

"The truth?" Sebastian laughed, the sound rich and hollow. "You destroyed a man's reputation because it sold more copies. Don't pretend it was about justice."

Heat crept up Seth's neck. The accusation stung because it carried some weight. He had to admit, his previous works had been calculated hit pieces, designed to capitalize on scandal and outrage. He needed the money at the time and that need outweighed the consequences of exposing the truth, hurtful or not. He always needed the money including this time. Why was he bucking his own system? Who cares about the truth when the fabrication pays a million dollars?

"You're right." Seth forced himself to meet Sebastian's gaze. "I chased sensationalism. But your story deserves better than that, right?"

Sebastian's expression softened. He pulled up a wooden chair, it creaked beneath his weight. "I knew you'd understand.

That's why I chose you, Seth. You recognize the value of a well-crafted narrative."

"Tell me about Constantinople." Seth opened his notebook, buying time to steady his nerves. "You mentioned being there during the fall?"

"Ah, yes." Sebastian leaned back, eyes distant. "The siege lasted fifty-three days. I watched from the Theodosian Walls as Mehmed's cannons reduced centuries of history to rubble. The air tasted of smoke and fear."

Seth's pen scratched across paper, recording details that couldn't possibly be firsthand knowledge. "But I wrote down earlier that you were in Târgoviște that same month. How could you be two placed at once?"

The temperature in the room seemed to drop. Sebastian's smile remained fixed, but something shifted behind his eyes. "My memory can sometimes be unreliable. After all, history is written by fallible men with limited perspectives."

"And which perspective should I write?" Seth's fingers tightened around his pen. "The one that matches history, or yours?"

"You're thinking like a journalist." Sebastian stood. "This isn't about facts and dates. It's about capturing the essence of an era, the feeling of standing at history's crossroads."

"What happened to Richard C. Morrison?" The question slipped out before he could stop it.

Sebastian's movement stilled. "I'm not familiar with the name."

"The true crime writer." Seth said. "He was working on a book about unexplained disappearances before he vanished himself."

"The world is full of unsolved mysteries." Sebastian's voice carried a ridged edge. "Writers often chase stories that lead nowhere. Some get lost in their own narratives. You know this do you not."

"I do." The hidden compartment creaked beneath Seth's foot. Sebastian's eyes flicked downward at the sound.

"Is something wrong with the floor?" Sebastian took a step closer.

Seth pushed back from the desk, forcing a casual shrug. "Old buildings have character. All these creaks and groans tell their own stories."

"Indeed they do." Sebastian placed a hand on Seth's shoulder, his grip just tight enough to suggest strength held in check. "Perhaps we should continue this discussion over dinner. I know an excellent restaurant in the village."

The invitation felt like a test. Or a trap. Seth thought of his girlfriend, of the wedding plans that hinged on this book's success.

"I'd like that." Seth stood, matching Sebastian's practiced smile. "Let me just pack up my notes."

Seth followed Sebastian through the penthouse's marble halls. Each step away from the library felt like abandoning a crime scene.

The elevator doors slid open with a soft chime. Sebastian gestured for Seth to enter first, a gesture that felt more threatening than courteous. The mirrored walls multiplied their reflections infinitely, like Seth's pale, drawn face and Sebastian's unchanging smile repeated into darkness.

"You seem distracted." Sebastian's voice filled the confined space. "Having doubts about the project?"

"Just processing everything." He briefly thought about pointing out Sabastian had a reflection in the mirrors but abandoned the idea to keep the peace. "Your story spans centuries. It's a lot to organize."

The elevator descended past floor after floor of Sebastian's private domain. Seth had never seen another resident, never heard sounds of life from behind the other doors. The whole building felt like a elaborate stage set, designed to project wealth and power while concealing something darker.

His phone vibrated again. Seth resisted the urge to check it, knowing another warning probably waited in his inbox. The anonymous tipster had impeccable timing, or was watching very closely.

The elevator stopped at the lobby. Sebastian's hand settled on Seth's shoulder, steering him toward the building's entrance. Outside, a black town car idled at the curb, its windows tinted to mirror darkness.

"I thought we might walk." Seth gestured toward the village lights glowing a few blocks away. "Clear my head, get some fresh air."

Sebastian's grip tightened fractionally. "The restaurant is too far. Get into the car. I insist."

Seth's stomach churned as the driver opened the rear door. The interior smelled of leather and something metallic, perhaps blood? No, his imagination was running wild.

"After you." Sebastian's smile hadn't wavered.

Seth slid across the leather seat, positioning himself behind the driver. If things went sideways, he'd have a better chance of reaching the door before Sebastian could react. The thought surprised him. When had he started planning escape routes?

The car pulled away from the curb. Seth watched Sebastian's reflection in the window, trying to reconcile the polished exterior with the evidence mounting against him. A centuries-old being who collected writers like butterflies, pinning their stories to the pages of hidden journals. His reflection gave him away. This was not a vampire, but he was a very wealthy and dangerous man.

"The chef is preparing something special tonight." Sebastian's voice cut through Seth's thoughts. "A traditional Romanian dish, one I haven't tasted for many years."

The car turned onto a darker street, moving away from the village lights. Seth's pulse quickened as unfamiliar buildings replaced the expected route.

"I thought Giovanni's was on Main Street?" Seth struggled to keep his voice steady.

"Change of plans." Sebastian's smile widened slightly. "I know a more private establishment. Somewhere we can discuss your... research methods in detail."

Seth's phone buzzed again. This time, he pulled it out, needing any distraction from the growing tension. The new message contained just three words: "Get out now."

The car slowed for a traffic light. Seth's hand found the door handle, his muscles tensing. Sebastian watched him with predatory focus, still wearing that perfect, unchanging smile. His eyes were fixed on Seth's hand on the handle.

"Going somewhere?" Sebastian's voice carried a hint of amusement.

Chapter 5
Emily Laurence

Seth forced his hand away from the door handle. "Just stretching." He pulled up his notes app instead of the warning message. "Actually, I'd love to hear more about your time in Romania. The historical context would add depth to the early chapters."

The traffic light turned green. Seth tracked their route through the window, cataloging each turn away from familiar streets. The buildings grew older, their facades weathered by decades of city grime. His stomach twisted as they passed beneath a broken streetlight, but he focused on his phone screen.

"What aspects interest you most?" Sebastian crossed his legs, the movement fluid and precise.

"The political climate during Vlad's reign. Your perspective on the Ottoman invasion would be invaluable." Seth typed quick notes, clinging to the familiar routine of research. "First-hand accounts from that period are rare."

"Indeed." Sebastian's reflection smiled in the darkened window. "Though history has a way of... sanitizing certain events. The real story is always more complex."

Seth's phone buzzed again. He swiped the notification away without reading it, diving deeper into his professional persona. "That's exactly why your biography could be groundbreaking. A fresh perspective on well-documented events."

The car turned down a narrow alley. Brick walls rose on either side, blocking out what little moonlight filtered through the clouds. Seth's pulse spiked, but he kept typing.

"Tell me about the night attack." The words tumbled out too fast. "The tactical advantages, the psychological impact on the Ottoman forces."

"Patience." Sebastian leaned forward. "Tonight is about building trust. You seem... distracted by outside influences."

Seth locked his phone, silencing the latest warning. "Just excited about the project. It's not every day you get to interview someone with your... historical knowledge."

The car emerged from the alley onto a wider street. Restored brownstones lined both sides, their windows glowing with warm light. Seth's shoulders relaxed fractionally as they pulled up to a townhouse with elegant ironwork and pristine white columns.

"Ah, here we are." Sebastian gestured to the building. "A private club, this is much better than some tourist-filled restaurant."

Seth stepped onto the sidewalk, shoving away thoughts of hidden journals and dead writers. The advance check had already been deposited. He'd committed to this project. Everything else was just imagination running wild after too many late nights researching vampire legends.

"Beautiful architecture." Seth pointed to the Victorian details above the door. "Original to the building?"

"Imported from London, actually. I supervised the restoration myself." Sebastian placed a hand on Seth's back, guiding him up the steps. "I find it's important to maintain connections to the past."

Seth focused on the craftsmanship, the historical significance, the potential chapters this location could inspire. He ignored the way Sebastian's hand felt like a brand through his jacket, the way the brass doorknob gleamed like fresh blood in the porch light.

"I'd love to include a section on your preservation work." Seth pulled out his phone again, creating a new note. "Your influence on the city's architectural heritage."

The door opened silently. Warm air carried the scent of old wood and expensive wine. Seth stepped into the foyer, mentally rewriting the evening's stakes. This wasn't a trap - it was a networking opportunity. Not a predator's lair, a chance to gather exclusive material for the biography.

He almost believed it.

Seth slumped in his chair at The Daily Grind, his laptop screen filled with half-written paragraphs about Sebastian's alleged time in Morocco. The coffee had gone cold, but he couldn't bring himself to order another. His bank account wouldn't thank him for it.

A flash of red caught his eye. A woman at the counter dropped her wallet, coins scattering across the floor. She crouched down, her dark curls falling forward as she reached for a quarter that had rolled under the display case.

"Here." Seth scooped up a handful of change. "If I were you, I'd keep that odd penny. It's from 1943. It's made of steel instead of copper and worth something to collectors."

She straightened up, green eyes crinkling at the corners. "A numismatist and a gentleman. That's not a combination you find every day in New York."

"More like a writer with too many random facts cluttering his brain." He handed over the coins. "I am full of useless trivia. He extended his hand, "Seth Aubrey."

"Emily Laurence." She shook his hand and then tucked the penny into her pocket instead of her wallet. "Writer? Should I know your work?"

Seth winced. "Unless you're into biographies of minor celebrities, probably not."

"Try me." She settled into the chair across from him, her coffee leaving a ring on his notes. "I read everything from cereal boxes to philosophical treatises."

"The Fallen Star: Senator Linda Morrison's Path to Obscurity?" Seth closed his laptop. "Or maybe Behind the Smile: The Real Trevor Banks?"

"The Trevor Banks expose?" Emily leaned forward. "That was you? I loved how you traced his charity foundation's money back to those offshore accounts."

Seth blinked. "You actually read it?"

"I'm an investigative journalist. Following paper trails is my idea of fun." She took a sip of coffee. "Though I have to ask. What made you switch from hard-hitting journalism to celebrity takedowns?"

"Bills." Seth shrugged. "I can't eat integrity."

"Fair enough." Emily pulled out her phone. "But you're wasting your talent. I'm working on a story about corporate tax evasion. I could use someone with your research skills."

Seth glanced at Sebastian's notes. "I'm actually in the middle of a project..."

"Pro bono, of course." Emily grinned. "But think of the exposure."

"Exposure doesn't pay rent."

"No, but dinner does." She slid her business card across the table. "Let me buy you a meal, pick your brain about investigative techniques. Maybe convince you to remember why you started writing in the first place."

Seth picked up the card. New York Times. His heart skipped. "I... yeah. Dinner would be great."

"Tomorrow? Seven?" Emily stood up, gathering her things. "There's this little Ethiopian place on 9th that makes incredible doro wat."

"I know it." Seth pocketed her card. "Though fair warning, my investigative techniques mostly involve coffee and stubbornness."

"What a coincidence, that's my favorite combination." She shouldered her bag. "Here, take the penny. Consider it a down payment on future collaborations." She took it from her pocket and slid it across the table to him. "Here give me your number and I'll send you a text with my info."

He gave her his number and she typed out a text, it sent from her phone with a swoop sound. She winked and left him there.

Seth watched her weave through the tables, her red sweater bright against the cafe's muted colors. He picked up the steel penny, turning it over in his fingers. For the first time in weeks, Sebastian's project felt less like an opportunity and more like a chain.

His phone buzzed, yet another text from an unknown number. He deleted it without reading, then pulled up Emily's contact information. His fingers hovered over the keyboard before typing: "Looking forward to tomorrow. I promise not to investigate your background before dinner."

Her reply came seconds later: "Already ran yours. Clean record, decent credit score, slight obsession with exposing other people's secrets. My kind of writer."

Seth laughed, earning strange looks from nearby customers. He turned back to his laptop, but Sebastian's story held no appeal. Instead, he opened a new document and began researching corporate tax structures. Just background information, he told himself. No harm in keeping his skills sharp.

He glanced at the penny sitting next to his cold coffee, its steel surface catching the afternoon light. He smiled and started typing.

Seth shuffled the biography notes across his desk, trying to focus on Sebastian's account of 18th century Vienna. His phone lit up with another message from Emily. He only glanced at it, something about a lead on offshore accounts. He smiled, then froze as Sebastian's voice cut through the penthouse study.

"New romance?" Sebastian stood behind Seth's chair, though Seth hadn't heard him approach. "She seems... intellectually stimulating."

Seth's fingers tightened on his phone. "Just a colleague. We're collaborating on some research. You know my girlfriend's name is Faith."

"Emily Laurence." Sebastian traced a finger along the desk's mahogany edge. He did that quite a lot and it set Seth's teeth on edge. "She graduated Columbia University, specializing in financial investigations. Recently, she has begun looking into certain private equity firms."

"How did you-"

"I make it my business to know who enters my biographer's life." Sebastian circled to face Seth. "Especially someone so... curious about other people's affairs."

Seth forced his breathing to remain steady. "Don't worry, the biography is my priority. Emily's story is just a side project."

"Of course." Sebastian's smile didn't reach his eyes. "Though I wonder if she knows about Faith."

"Of course not. Why would I tell a colleague I just met about my girlfriend?"

"Why wouldn't you. Normally, people mention their significant other to curb any romantic feelings or to at least let them know they are already taken. You did neither, which means you are interested in more than just Emily's side story."

"Well, I don't actually mind telling her. It just never came up."

"Oh, and what if it does come up? What would happen then?"

"I would tell her, of course. Why all the questioning?"

"Did I strike a nerve? Are you sure her work isn't going to become distracting?"

"Nothing that would interfere with your biography." Seth pulled up his outline. "Actually, I'd love your perspective on Maria Theresa's court. Your description of the Winter Palace."

"I don't share well, Seth." Sebastian placed a hand on Seth's shoulder. Cold seeped through his shirt. "My story requires your complete attention. Distractions could prove... unfortunate."

"Emily's just a friend." Seth opened a new document. "Now, about the Habsburg dynasty..."

"Excellent choice." Sebastian's grip loosened. "Though perhaps we should discuss this over dinner. I know an intimate little place in the Village. They do not allow cell phones. Perfect for maintaining focus."

Seth nodded, already calculating how many chapters he needed to complete before he could safely distance himself from this project. The advance would keep him afloat while he built his investigative career back up. He just had to play along, stick to safe topics, keep Emily separate from all this. Sabastian was quick to make him understand how dangerous he was to cross.

He would have to be careful not to make him feel threatened by another project.

"Let me grab my coat." Seth stood, careful not to brush against Sebastian.

"A wise decision." Sebastian gestured toward the door. "I find loyalty is richly rewarded. And Seth?" His eyes gleamed in the dim light. "Do give Ms. Laurence my regards."

Seth swallowed hard and followed Sebastian out of the study, leaving his phone face-down on the desk. Just a few more months of research, then he'd be free to pursue his own stories again.

Chapter 6
An Ill-Conceived Decision

Seth's fingers hovered over the keyboard. Another writer, James C. Morrison, no relation to Senator Linda Morrison, had attempted Sebastian's biography five years ago. The thought nagged at him through sleepless nights until he couldn't ignore it anymore. He opened a new browser tab and typed Morrison's name.

Obituaries filled the screen. Found in his Manhattan apartment, apparent heart attack at forty-two. No history of cardiac issues. The dates aligned perfectly. He died three months after signing with Sebastian, according to the journal in the hidden spot in the floor he had sneaked another peek at when Sabastian was out.

Seth clicked through archived social media posts. Morrison's excitement about a "dream project" gave way to scattered updates about "strange discoveries" and "historical inconsistencies." The final post stood out: "Some stories should stay buried. Getting out while I can."

Two days later, Morrison was dead.

Seth dug deeper. Morrison's apartment had been cleaned out before police arrived. His computer had been completely wiped, and his papers and notes were all gone. The only item of note was an antique leather journal, dismissed as research material. The same journal Seth had found hidden in Sebastian's library.

His phone buzzed. It was Emily asking about dinner plans. He closed the tabs and promised to meet her in an hour. But first, he needed answers.

The university library's microfiche archives held copies of Morrison's earlier work. Seth scrolled through articles, looking for anything about Sebastian. In the corner of a society page photo, he spotted Morrison at a charity gala. Sebastian stood in the background, unchanged from today. The photo was dated 1987.

Seth's hands shook as he printed the image. The date had to be wrong. Sebastian looked exactly the same, not just similar, but identical. Even his suit style matched his current taste.

A librarian's cart squeaked behind him. "Finding everything okay?"

Seth jumped, shoving the printout into his bag. "Yes, thanks. Just finishing up."

More searches revealed Morrison's other articles mentioning Sebastian. Each time, buried in society pages or business profiles, that same unchanging face appeared. The dates on the photos Morrison had dug up went back further. They included the years 1975, 1968, and 1954.

Seth's phone buzzed again. Emily. He was late.

In his rush to pack up, a yellowed newspaper clipping fluttered to the floor. Morrison's final published piece. It contained an obituary for another writer, David Chenowith. "Promising biographer found dead in his home." The article mentioned Chenowith's upcoming book about a "reclusive business figure."

Seth's throat went dry. Chenowith had been Sebastian's biographer before Morrison. The pattern stretched back every few years, a writer disappeared or died suddenly. Their unfinished manuscripts vanished. Police investigations led nowhere.

The library lights flickered overhead. Closing time. Seth gathered his evidence. The facts formed a horrible picture: Sebastian chose writers, used them to craft his story, then eliminated loose ends.

His phone lit up with Emily's third message. Seth stared at her smiling profile photo, remembering Sebastian's too-detailed knowledge of her schedule, her clothes. The threat felt suddenly, terribly real.

He needed to get to Emily, but first, he wanted to find Sebastian.

Seth burst into Sebastian's penthouse. The elevator doors closed behind him with a soft chime that echoed through the vast space.

"I know what happened to Morrison. And Chenowith." Seth's voice escalated. "All of them."

Sebastian lounged in his leather armchair, crystal glass in hand. The amber liquid within caught the light as he swirled it. "Do you? Please, enlighten me."

"The deaths. The disappearances. Every few years, another writer." Seth pulled out the printouts. "And you. You're in all these photos. Decades apart, but you haven't aged a day."

"Ah." Sebastian set down his glass. "Come here. Let me show you something."

Seth's curiosity carried him forward despite his instincts screaming to run. Sebastian led him to a previously hidden alcove where a small painting hung. It depicted a Renaissance piece showing a man in agony, his hands severed at the wrists.

"Giovanni Rossi. Brilliant artist in Florence, 1547." Sebastian's voice took on a storyteller's cadence. "He painted the most exquisite portraits. Captured not just appearances, but souls. The wealthy fought for his commissions."

Seth's mouth went dry. "What happened to him?"

"He painted my portrait. He noticed, as you did, certain... inconsistencies. Rather than keep our arrangement, he became obsessed with exposing the truth." Sebastian focused on the frame. "He began asking questions and making accusations. He threatened to reveal what he'd learned."

"They cut off his hands?"

"I did." Sebastian's casual tone turned Seth's blood to ice. "A fitting punishment for an artist who couldn't honor his commitments. The official story blamed rival painters, of course. Politics were nasty in Renaissance Florence."

"Why are you telling me this?"

"Because you're at a crossroads, Seth. Like Giovanni. Like Morrison. Like all the others who couldn't simply tell the story they were paid to tell." Sebastian picked up his glass again. "I find it helps to provide... historical context. Perspective on the choices before you. Wouldn't you say it was a rather dumb idea to approach me with such accusations? You do have some courage. I like that."

Seth backed away. The painting's subject stared at him with eyes full of terror and regret. "You're insane."

"I'm practical. Stories shape reality, Seth. The storyteller wields immense power. That's why I choose my biographers carefully, and why I deal decisively with those who prove... unreliable."

"The journal I found-"

"Belonged to Morrison. As did the one before it, and the one before that. I keep them as reminders." Sebastian's smile again didn't reach his eyes. There was no sincerity in it. "Each writer adds their own perspective before meeting their end. It's quite the collection."

Seth thought of Emily waiting at the restaurant, checking her phone. His research scattered across his apartment. The evidence he'd gathered. He was disgusted with himself, but Sabastian was right. This was a stupid idea, confronting him.

"I won't tell anyone," Seth whispered. "I'll write whatever story you want."

"Of course you will." Sebastian gestured to the painting. At first, "Giovanni said the same thing. They all did. But curiosity is such a dangerous trait in a writer. The questions never really stop, do they?"

The painting's mutilated subject bore witness to centuries of similar conversations, similar threats. His throat closed around unspoken questions, each one a potential death sentence.

"I need air." Seth stumbled toward the penthouse's glass doors. The Manhattan skyline blurred through cold sweat and rising panic.

Sebastian returned to his chair, watching with predatory patience. "Take all the time you need. The terrace offers an excellent view for... contemplation."

The night air hit Seth's face like a slap. Forty stories below, yellow cabs crawled through gridlocked streets. Normal people living normal lives, unaware of the monster in their midst. His fingers gripped the railing until his knuckles went white.

Facts arranged themselves with brutal clarity. Sebastian was immortal, or something close to it. He killed writers who discovered his secret. Seth had discovered his secret. The math wasn't complicated.

Seth pressed his forehead against the cold metal railing. The choice crystallized: risk death by staying, or guarantee ruin by leaving. Behind him, Sebastian's silhouette remained motionless, waiting.

A memory surfaced, Emily laughing at his paranoid theories about previous assignments. "You always think everyone's hiding something terrible. Sometimes a story is just a story."

Maybe that was the answer. Stop digging. Write the authorized version. Focus on Sebastian's business empire, his philanthropy, his carefully curated public image. Ignore the photographs that spanned decades. Forget Chenowith and Morrison's fate.

Play along. Stay alive.

Seth straightened, smoothed his jacket. Through the glass, Sebastian raised his glass in silent acknowledgment. The message was clear. His continued cooperation bought survival, for now.

"I understand the parameters." Seth kept his voice steady as he reentered the penthouse. "The official biography. Nothing more. I'll just continue with the work at hand."

"Excellent." Sebastian's smile showed too many teeth. "I knew you were the right choice. You see the bigger picture."

Seth nodded, already planning. He'd back up his research somewhere secure and then set a dead man's switch on his email. Insurance, in case Sebastian's promises proved as immortal as their maker. All he had to do was write the biography as instructed and then he could get away from this monster.

"One question." Seth forced himself to meet those ancient eyes. "Why me?"

"Your previous work shows such... insight into human nature. The ability to find the story beneath the story." Sebastian swirled his drink. "Though perhaps a bit too much insight, at times."

The compliment carried poison. Seth's reputation for exposing secrets had attracted Sebastian's attention and now threatened to become his death warrant. Every skill that made him valuable made him dangerous.

"I should get going. I need to begin organizing my notes." Seth edged toward the elevator. "Besides, Emily's waiting." He flinched at the words. He had not meant to say her name in Sabastian's presence.

"Ah yes, the lovely Emily." Sebastian's gaze sharpened. "Do give her my regards."

Seth's finger jabbed the elevator button. The doors opened with merciful speed. He maintained composure until they closed, then sagged against the wall. His reflection showed a face aged years in hours.

The choice was made. He would write Sebastian's story, at least the public version, and keep his head down. He would keep his questions to himself and stay alive.

But he would also prepare. He would have to protect himself, Faith, and Emily. Some stories had to stay buried, but that didn't mean they couldn't be weaponized. What was to keep Sabastian from disposing of him anyway when the work was done? He had to have a contingency plan.

Seth pulled out his phone as the elevator descended. Emily's worried messages filled the screen. He typed quickly: "Sorry, meeting ran long. On my way. Everything's fine."

The lie felt like the first of many to come.

Chapter 7
The Next Step

Seth hunched over his laptop in the back corner of a dimly lit coffee shop. The place smelled of burnt espresso and desperation, which was fitting for what his life had become. Three weeks since his confrontation with Sebastian, and he'd managed to produce exactly five sanitized pages of biography that wouldn't get him killed.

The bell above the door jingled. Seth glanced up, then immediately back down at his screen. Just another customer seeking caffeine, not Sebastian or any of his minions coming to ensure his compliance.

"Vanilla latte for Pike," called the barista.

A thin man with wire-rimmed glasses approached the counter. His clothes hung loose on his frame, and his eyes darted nervously around the room. When his gaze landed on Seth, he froze.

Seth shifted uncomfortably. The man grabbed his drink and, instead of leaving, walked directly toward Seth's table.

"Mr. Aubrey?" The man's voice barely carried over the coffee shop's ambient noise.

Seth closed his laptop. "Yes? Do I know you?"

"No, but I know you." The man slid into the chair opposite Seth without invitation. "Nathan Pike. I've been trying to reach you."

Seth's pulse quickened. The anonymous warnings. "You're the one who has been texting me?"

Nathan nodded, his eyes constantly scanning the room. "It's not safe to talk here. He has people everywhere."

"Sebastian," Seth whispered. "You know him?"

Nathan flinched at the name. "Fifty years I served him. I watched what he did to people like you." His fingers trembled around his cup. "Writers, mostly. Anyone who got too close to the truth. I don't think you understand what you have gotten yourself into."

Seth leaned forward. "Why are you telling me this?"

"Because you're different." Nathan's voice strengthened. "You found Morrison's journal. You know what's coming, but you're still here."

"I don't have much choice."

"There's always a choice." Nathan reached into his worn messenger bag and withdrew a leather-bound book. "This belonged to his last servant before me. Winston Shaw. He documented everything, the killings, the manipulation, the centuries of... atrocities. Here, I want you to have it."

Seth stared at the journal. Its edges were worn smooth, the leather cracked with age. "Why give this to me?"

"Because you're a storyteller. Because you know how to make people believe." Nathan pushed the journal across the table. "And because I need someone to understand what will happen if Sebastian isn't stopped."

Seth didn't touch the book. "He'll kill me if I try to expose him."

"He'll kill you anyway." Nathan's matter-of-fact tone sent ice through Seth's veins. "Once your book is finished, you're just another loose end, just like Morrison and Chenowith, just like all the others."

Seth's fingers hovered over the journal. "What happened to Winston?"

"Sebastian caught him writing this." Nathan tapped the journal. "He made me watch what he did. He said it was a lesson in loyalty." His eyes unfocused, seeing something Seth couldn't. "Three days it took. Three days for Winston to die."

Seth pulled his hand back. "I can't. I have people. I have to think of Emily, my girlfriend Faith—"

"He already knows about them." Nathan's voice dropped lower. "He's just waiting to see which one you care about more before he uses them against you."

The coffee in Seth's stomach turned to acid. "What do you expect me to do with this?"

"Read it. Learn from it." Nathan stood, adjusting his bag. "There's a way to stop him, but you need to understand what you're facing first."

Seth reluctantly took the journal. It looked nondescript and harmless. "How do I contact you?"

"You don't. I'll find you." Nathan's eyes darted to the window. His face drained of color. "He's early."

Seth turned. A black town car had pulled up outside. "Sebastian?"

"No. One of his watchers." Nathan went back toward the service exit. "Read the journal. Burn it when you're done. I don't care. Trust no one who's been near him—they're either his or they're dead."

"How did you escape him?" Seth asked.

"Just read the journal and learn from it. I'll be in touch."

Before Seth could respond, Nathan slipped through the kitchen and disappeared. Seconds later, a broad-shouldered man in an expensive suit entered the coffee shop. His eyes swept the room, pausing briefly on Seth before moving on.

Seth shoved the journal into his laptop bag and gathered his things. He steadied the tremor in his hand as he paid his bill, feeling the suited man's gaze tracking his movements.

Outside, Seth walked briskly away from the coffee shop, fighting the urge to run. He couldn't wait to get somewhere safe where he could examine it. Nathan's warning echoed in his mind: "He'll kill you anyway."

His phone buzzed with a text from Sebastian: "Looking forward to reviewing your progress tomorrow. 8 PM. Don't be late."

Seth clutched his bag tighter.

Seth entered Sebastian's penthouse. Winston's journal remained safely hidden in his apartment. Because of the journal, he knew what Sabastian was now. He knew about the vampire's victims through centuries, each dispatched with calculated cruelty after serving their purpose. Winston suspected the vampire got his sustenance from more than just blood.

"Ah, Seth." Sebastian emerged from the shadows of his study, moving with that unnatural grace. "I trust you've made progress?"

"Five chapters drafted." Seth kept his voice steady as he handed over the pages. "Your early years in San Antonio, military service, and the transformation."

Sebastian's cold fingers brushed against Seth's as he took the pages. "All according to our agreed narrative, I presume?"

"Exactly as you described." Seth forced himself to meet those ancient eyes. "Nothing... extra."

"Excellent." Sebastian gestured toward the leather chairs. "Drink?"

"No, thank you." Seth remained standing. Every instinct screamed to maintain distance.

Sebastian hesitated before he read the pages, "You seem tense tonight. Perhaps you're working too hard?" He circled behind Seth, movements fluid as water. "Or perhaps you've been... distracted."

Seth's mouth went dry. "Just deadline pressure."

"Hmm." Sebastian's voice came from directly behind him. "And how is the lovely Emily? Still pursuing her financial investigations?"

Seth's pulse jumped. "She's fine. She's working on them. I don't know much more about it. I have been busy with my own project." He indicated the pages Sabastian held in his hands.

"I saw her yesterday, you know." Sebastian moved to the window, gazing out at the city lights. "Outside the Times building. That red coat suits her. Brings out the warmth in her skin."

Ice slid down Seth's spine. "You were watching her?"

"I observe many things, Seth." Sebastian turned, his expression pleasant but his eyes flat. "Your apartment building. Emily's office. Your girlfriend Faith's dance studio."

Seth's fists clenched involuntarily.

"Did you know Faith cries in her car after class?" Sebastian's tone remained conversational. "Three nights this week. She suspects something, doesn't she? About you and Emily?"

"There's nothing—"

"Please." Sebastian waved a dismissive hand. "I can smell her on you. Your loyalties are... divided." He stepped closer. "I don't appreciate divided loyalties, Seth."

"My personal life doesn't affect our work."

"Everything affects our work." Sebastian glanced at Seth's manuscript. "These pages are adequate but lacking the... passion of your previous writing. I wonder where that passion has gone?"

Seth swallowed. "I'll work harder."

"See that you do." Sebastian's lips curled into a thin smile. "I would hate for anything to happen to either of those lovely women in your life while you're distracted with... other matters."

The threat hung in the air between them. Seth nodded stiffly, his eyes fixed on a point ahead of him instead of Sabastian. He knew if he met his gaze, the vampire would see the contempt in his eyes.

"Eight o'clock tomorrow." Sebastian walked to the door, signaling the meeting's end. "Bring the next chapters. And Seth?" His voice dropped to a near whisper. "Choose your priorities carefully. Not everyone in your life can remain there."

He turned once he was in the elevator, "What's that supposed to mean." Seth couldn't help himself.

"I am just saying things, as well as circumstances, change."

The elevator doors closed on Sebastian's predatory smile. Seth sagged against the wall, sweat beading on his forehead. The message couldn't have been clearer – Sebastian knew everything and would use anyone to keep Seth in line.

Emily's apartment smelled of curry and jasmine. Seth paced her small living room.

"You look terrible." Emily handed him a glass of wine. "Sebastian again?"

Seth took a long swallow. "He's watching you."

"What?"

"He described your red coat. Knew you were at the Times building yesterday." Seth set the glass down with shaking hands. "He's watching Faith too."

Emily's face hardened. "That manipulative bastard."

"It's worse than that." Seth pulled her away from the window. "He's dangerous, Emily. The things I've found—"

She pressed her fingers to his lips. "Not here. Walls have ears, remember?"

Seth nodded. They'd already swept her apartment for bugs twice, but paranoia had become their baseline.

Emily led him to the bathroom, turned on the shower, and sat on the edge of the tub. "Talk."

Seth told her everything. He filled her in on Winston's journal, and the centuries of murdered writers, as well as Sebastian's thinly veiled threats.

"We need to go to the police." Emily's voice was firm.

"With what? A journal from a dead man describing a vampire?" Seth shook his head. "They'd laugh us out of the precinct."

"Then we gather more evidence." She took his hands. "Together."

The shower steam fogged the mirror, shrouding them in artificial mist.

"Emily, do you believe in vampires?"

"I do now. In Winst0n's journal he says he feeds off more than blood. What if it's human misery. Just like you, he has basically tortured all his biographers."

"A vampire who commissions biographies never to have them published, but instead using them as a way to cause misery?"

"Yeah."

Seth nodded, "It's something to think about. He does seem to thrive on it."

Emily turned his head, forcing him to look her in the eye, "You can't keep living like this." Her voice softened. "Lying to Faith, hiding from Sebastian, carrying all this alone."

"I don't know what else to do." Seth's shoulders slumped.

Emily's lips found his, hesitant at first, then hungry. The kiss deepened, her hands sliding under his shirt, pressing against his skin.

"Emily—" he gasped.

"I know." She pulled back slightly. "It's complicated with Faith and all."

"I need to end things with her." The words tumbled out. "It's not fair to keep stringing her along. Not when I feel this way about you."

Emily searched his eyes, "Are you sure? This isn't just the stress or—"

"I've never been surer of anything." Seth pulled her close again. "Whatever happens with Sebastian, I can't keep lying to her. To myself."

Emily's body pressed against his, the shower steam wrapping around them like a cocoon. For a moment, the danger receded, replaced by something more electric and urgent.

"Tomorrow," Seth whispered against her neck. "I'll talk to Faith tomorrow."

Faith's apartment was quiet when Seth arrived the next evening. Her dance shoes lay neatly by the door, her favorite mug still warm on the counter. The faint scent of her perfume lingered in the air, making what he came to do even more difficult. He shifted his weight from one foot to the other, rehearsing the words he'd practiced on the subway ride over.

"You're early." She emerged from the bedroom, hair damp from the shower, wearing the blue cotton robe he'd given her last Christmas. "I was just—" She stopped, reading his expression. Her smile faded, replaced with concern. "What's wrong?"

Seth took a deep breath, his stomach knotting with guilt. Emily's face flashed in his mind. "We need to talk," he said, hating how cliché the words sounded even as they left his mouth.

He left Faith crying in her apartment. He felt like a heel. He rode the elevator down to the ground floor. When the doors opened a woman in white almost ran smack into him as he stepped off the elevator. "Oh, excuse me," he said.

Her face remained stoic, "Are you going to get off so I can get on or are you just going to stand there?"

Seth stepped aside as the woman got on the elevator. She turned to face him as the doors closed. Her eyes never left contact with his. She gave him a shiver.

Chapter 8
Fear and Truth

On impulse, Seth pressed the up button and waited for the elevator to return. He rode it back up to Faith's floor. When he stepped off, he saw the woman enter Faith's apartment. He quickened his step to go after her. What if Sabastian sent her. He got to the door. She was no longer crying. The woman was speaking. She was saying something about the White Covenant, whatever that was. Faith offered her a drink. She was fine. Seth went back to the elevator.

He left the building and stood watching the people walking beneath the streetlights. The breakup had been clean but painful, like removing a bullet without anesthesia. Her final words echoed in his mind: "I hope she's worth whatever you're going through."

He checked his watch. Three hours until his meeting with Sebastian. Just enough time to make a stop that wouldn't appear on any schedule the vampire might be monitoring.

The university library basement smelled of dust and old books. Perfect. Seth nodded to the elderly archivist who barely looked up from her crossword puzzle as he slipped into the microfilm room.

He loaded the first reel. The label read obituaries from 1978. If Sebastian had been eliminating biographers for centuries, there had to be patterns. Common elements. Weaknesses. He hoped to find something that would give him a clue as how to protect himself it worse came to worse.

"Looking for something specific?"

Seth nearly jumped out of his skin. A young woman with thick glasses and a cardigan stood in the doorway.

"Just... research." He positioned himself to block the screen.

"On Marco Chenowith?" She stepped closer, peering around him. "The writer David Chenowith's father? That's quite the coincidence."

Seth's pulse quickened. "You know about Chenowith?"

"My grandmother worked with him." She extended her hand. "Connie Stone. And you're Seth Aubrey, Sebastian's newest project."

Seth tensed, ready to bolt, but Connie raised her hands. "Relax. I'm not one of *his*. Quite the opposite."

"How did you find me?"

"I've been tracking his pattern for years." Connie pulled up a chair. "Every biographer, every journalist who gets too close. My grandmother was David Chenowith's research assistant.

Sebastian destroyed her after Chenowith die. Not physically, but..." She tapped her temple. "He took everything that made her herself."

Seth studied her face, looking for deception. "Why are you telling me this?"

"Because you're still alive." She pulled a flash drive from her pocket. "Which means you're either exceptionally careful or exceptionally valuable to him."

"Or exceptionally stupid." Seth took the drive. "What's this?"

"Everything I've compiled. Names, dates, patterns." Connie glanced toward the door. "There are others like us. You know, people who've lost someone to him. We keep track of each other. We stay mostly hidden. I'd like to tell you more, but it's too soon. I think we should get to know each other though."

Seth slipped the drive into his pocket. "How do I know I can trust you?"

"You don't. But we're running out of time." She scribbled a number on a scrap of paper. "Use this if you find something or if he suspects. Memorize it, then destroy it. We may be what you are seeking. We may have the ability to help you survive this ordeal."

"What do you know about it."

Connie looked at him bemused, "Haven't you been listening? I know everything about it."

Seth studied Connie's face, still unsure whether or not to trust or believe her, but her eyes remained steady behind those thick glasses. There was something else there, a haunted quality that resonated with his own growing fear.

"You're in more danger than you realize," she said, lowering her voice to barely above a whisper. "Sebastian isn't just watching you. He's preparing."

"Preparing for what?" Seth asked, his throat dry.

"For whatever comes after your usefulness ends." Connie glanced toward the library's entrance. "The biography is just a means to an end. He uses them to rewrite his own history, to cover his tracks."

"Does he feed off them? I mean the writing of them?"

Connie's face contorted into one of shock and surprise, "aren't you full of surprises. You do know more than I thought."

"Does he?"

"I think you already know the answer to that question."

Seth thought of the sanitized chapters he'd written, the carefully constructed narrative that painted Sebastian as a mysterious but ultimately benevolent figure. "I've been helping him."

"They all did, at first." Connie leaned closer. "But I have friends, powerful friends who might be able to help you, if you keep an open mind and stay alive."

"What kind of friends?" Seth asked, skepticism creeping into his voice despite his desperation. "Law enforcement? Journalists?"

Connie's lips curved into a humorless smile. "People with experience dealing with Sebastian's... kind. People who've been hunting them for generations."

"Hunting vampires?" The words sounded ridiculous even as Seth whispered them. Yet after everything he'd seen, everything he'd learned from Winston's journal, could he really dismiss anything?

"I know how it sounds," she said, as if reading his thoughts. "But you've seen enough to know this isn't normal. Sebastian isn't human, and he hasn't been for centuries."

Seth breathed in deeply. "Not just since World War II" He smiled.

"His standard insistence even though he tells stories from much earlier in history." She laughed. "

"Why does he do that?"

"Who knows."

"How do I contact these friends of yours?" he asked.

Connie checked her watch, a nervous habit that reminded Seth of his own growing paranoia. "That flash drive has an encrypted messaging app. Instructions are in a text file. Memorize them, then destroy the file."

"Why would they help me?"

"Because you're inside his circle. You have access none of us have had in decades." She glanced around the library again, her movements becoming more agitated. "And because stopping Sebastian matters more than any one of us."

Seth pocketed the flash drive. "What about Emily? And Faith? They're both in danger because of me."

"We can help them too, but you need to be careful. Sebastian's been watching you for longer than you think." Connie stood abruptly. "We have a strict ten-minute rule for talking in public. It's dangerous to stay connected too long."

"Your friends have a ten-minute rule? Wait—" Seth reached for her arm. "How do you know all this? Who are you really?"

Connie hesitated, then pulled back her sleeve to reveal a jagged scar running from wrist to elbow. "Sebastian doesn't just kill writers. Sometimes he keeps people for his own entertainment, for blood, for information. My mother was one of his 'companions' for seven years. When she tried to escape with me, he found us." Her voice hardened. "I was eleven. I've spent every day since learning how to fight him. When the time is right, I will introduce you to the rest. For now, I have to go."

"I'll contact you," he promised.

Connie nodded once, sharply. "Remember—ten minutes, maximum in public. Any longer and his people might notice patterns." She shouldered her bag and headed for the exit, then paused. "One more thing. If he offers you anything, immortality, wealth, protection, you must refuse it."

Then she was gone, disappearing between the tall library shelves with practiced efficiency. He sat alone at the microfilm reader. He checked his pocket to make sure the flash drive was still there. It was.

"The chapter on my time in Vienna lacks authenticity." Sebastian tossed the pages onto his desk. "You've written about historical events any researcher could find, not my personal experiences."

Seth maintained his carefully neutral expression. "I'm still getting a feel for your voice. The emotional texture."

"Hmm." Sebastian circled behind him, a predator assessing weakness. "And how was your conversation with Faith? Emotional, I imagine?"

Seth's stomach suddenly felt queasy. Of course Sebastian knew. "It was necessary."

"Clearing the path for Emily?" Sebastian's breath was cold against Seth's neck. "Or clearing distractions from our work?"

"Both." Seth met Sebastian's gaze steadily. "You were right. Divided loyalties complicate things." He thought briefly about lying and saying there was no interest in Emily, but he figured the vampire probably already knew about that too.

Sebastian's lips curled into a satisfied smile. "I'm pleased you're beginning to understand what's important."

Seth nodded, playing the role of the cowed writer. Inside, he tried not to dwell too long on the information on Connie's flash drive, made up of several accounts of Sebastian's victims spanning decades, all documenting the same pattern of seduction, manipulation, and disposal for fear he might be able to read his mind somehow or see the deceptive knowledge in the folds of his expressions.

"I need more details about Vienna," Seth said, redirecting the conversation. "The emotional texture, as you said. Perhaps if you showed me something personal from that period? A keepsake, a letter?"

Sebastian studied him for a long moment. "Your curiosity is admirable, if potentially dangerous."

"I just want to get it right." Seth adopted an eager expression. "The biography you deserve."

"Very well." Sebastian led him to a hidden panel in the library wall. "Perhaps these will inspire you."

The compartment contained a small wooden box. Inside lay yellowed letters tied with faded ribbon, and beneath them, a daguerreotype of a young woman.

"Elsa Brenner," Sebastian's voice softened with what sounded like genuine emotion. "A pianist at the Vienna Opera. She had the most extraordinary hands."

Seth carefully examined the items, noting details while appearing appropriately awed. The date on one letter, 1842, matched information from Connie's files about a missing musician.

"She must have been special," Seth murmured.

"She was." Sebastian closed the box abruptly. "Until she wasn't."

The threat lingered in the air between them. Seth nodded with understanding. He was useful to Sebastian. Until he wasn't.

"I found three more." Emily's voice was muffled against Seth's chest as they lay tangled in her sheets. "Writers who disappeared after contact with Sebastian. All their work vanished too."

"Not completely if you found something."

She playfully punched him, "You know what I mean."

Seth ran his index finger down her bare shoulder. "Connie's network identified two in Paris and one in Buenos Aires. All with the same pattern."

"We're building a case." Emily propped herself up on one elbow. "But for what? Who would believe us?"

"Not about what he is." Seth tucked a strand of hair behind her ear. "About what he's done. The financial crimes, the disappearances. We can build a case about the things he's done that doesn't require believing in vampires."

Emily kissed him softly. "You're getting good at this. You're almost thinking like him."

"I have to." Seth pulled her closer. "It's the only way to stay ahead of him."

"Just don't lose yourself in the process." Emily's fingers traced the worry lines on his forehead. "I didn't fall for a manipulative predator. I fell for the man who wants to expose the truth."

Seth smiled. For the first time in weeks, he felt something like hope. Sebastian had centuries of experience and supernatural abilities, but Seth had something the vampire couldn't understand—a network of people united by loss, and a partner who saw through his facades to the truth beneath.

Emily rolled onto her back, staring at the ceiling fan spinning lazily above them. The morning light filtered through her half-drawn blinds.

"What's he like?" she asked suddenly. "Sebastian. When you're alone with him."

Seth tensed. The question seemed to come from nowhere, disrupting the peaceful moment they'd been sharing. "Why do you want to know?"

"Professional curiosity." Emily turned to face him. "You're writing his biography. I'm wondering what kind of man hires someone to document his life."

Seth chose his words carefully. "He's... intense. Always watching, analyzing. Like he's cataloging every reaction, every word."

"Handsome?" Emily rubbed her fingers absently on his chest.

"I guess women would think so." Seth frowned. "Classical features. Dark hair. Tall."

"You sound jealous." Emily smiled, but something in her expression worried him.

"I'm not jealous. I'm concerned." Seth sat up, the sheet pooling around his waist. "Why the sudden interest in what he looks like?"

Emily shrugged. "Just trying to picture the man who's taken over your life. Is his voice hypnotically deep or high and scratchy?"

She smiled mischievously and Seth got the joke. She wasn't serious about the sound of his voice. "You're just messing with me now."

"You think?" Emily waved dismissively. "Jealously doesn't suit you."

Seth studied her face. Her expression remained jovial, but there was something in her eyes, perhaps a hunger for information that hadn't been there before. Or had he simply not noticed it? "Do you really want to know?

"Sure, why not?"

"His voice is... Distinctive. Old-fashioned cadence. I guess you would say it's deep enough to persuade. Is that what you wanted to know?"

"Yeah, I mean nothing by it. I'm Just curious about the monster you're dealing with." She sat up beside him. "Does he ever talk about his past? His real past, not the sanitized version?"

Seth pulled away slightly. "Sometimes. Fragments. Vienna in the 1800s. Renaissance Florence."

She grinned. "You spend more time with him than with me these days."

"That's not fair. I'm trying to stay alive, to protect us both." Seth got out of bed, suddenly needing distance. "And now you're asking about his appearance, his voice, I can't tell if you really want to know this stuff or if you're just messing with me and it's uncomfortable."

"Oh, relax, I'm just curious. Again, I don't mean anything by it."

Seth wanted to believe her, he needed to believe her. But Winston's journal had described how Sebastian seduced his victims. He didn't act upon them just physically, but also mentally. How he created fascination before moving in for the kill.

"Has he contacted you in some way?" Seth asked.

"What? No!" Emily got out of bed, wrapping the sheet around herself. "Seth, listen to yourself. You're becoming even more paranoid."

"What do you mean becoming? You already know I am. He makes you this way, uncertain, paranoid."

Emily approached him slowly, like he was a spooked animal. "No one has contacted me. I'm asking questions because I care about you, because I want to understand what you're facing."

She placed her hands on his chest, her warm touch pressing against his skin. "I'm on your side, Seth. Always."

Seth wanted to believe her. The alternative was too painful to consider. It would be completely believable for him to start grooming Emily. A sudden fear gripped him, with Faith now out of the picture, Nathan Pike's words came to him. *He is just waiting to see which one is more important to you, so he knows who to use against you, or something like that.*

"I'm sorry." He exhaled slowly. "This whole situation has me seeing threats everywhere."

"I know." Emily stood on tiptoe, pressing her lips to his. The kiss deepened, her body melting against his.

Seth's doubts receded as her hands moved down his chest, her touch erasing his concerns. Her kiss grew more insistent, more passionate, driving thoughts of Sebastian from his mind.

When they finally broke apart, Emily looked up at him with clear and focused eyes. "Better?"

Seth nodded, his earlier suspicions seeming ridiculous now. "Much better."

"Good." Emily smiled. "No more talk of vampires this morning. We have better things to do."

Chapter 9
Small Victories

Seth's fingers trembled as he fitted his key into the lock. The day had been long, the meeting with Sebastian even longer, and all he wanted was a hot shower and sleep. The key turned, but the door swung open too easily, as if already unlocked.

He froze. He always locked his door. Always.

The apartment beyond lay in shadows, but even in the dim light spilling from the hallway, Seth could see something was wrong. Papers scattered across the floor. Drawers pulled open. Couch cushions slashed and tossed aside.

His throat tightened. Someone had been here. Someone had searched his place.

Seth flipped on the light switch and surveyed the damage. His laptop remained untouched on the desk. Good thing he'd taken to carrying the hard drive separately in his pocket, smart move.

The television still hung on the wall, his watch collection sat undisturbed. It was not a robbery, then.

"Sebastian," he whispered, the name like acid on his tongue.

He moved cautiously through the wreckage of his living room into the bedroom. The mattress had been flipped, clothes dumped from drawers. They'd been thorough. But not thorough enough.

Seth knelt beside his bed frame, fingers finding the small gap where the wood joined the metal. Winston's journal remained secure in its hiding place, wrapped in plastic and duct tape. His stash of research notes were similarly untouched. He had distributed them across three different locations Connie had helped him secure.

A grim satisfaction settled in his chest. Sebastian's people had found nothing.

His phone buzzed. A text from an unknown number: "Safe?"

Connie. Seth typed back: "Yes. Apartment searched. Everything secure."

The reply came seconds later: "New location ready. Address follows. Destroy after memorizing."

Seth committed the address to memory, then deleted the conversation. He surveyed his violated home once more before grabbing an overnight bag. He couldn't stay here. He finished packing and headed for the door. Connie would help him lie low for a few days. She would even help him stay in touch with Emily, although he made it a point not to tell Emily about her or the victim's network, just in case.

"You've been busy." Connie pushed a steaming mug of coffee across the table toward him.

They sat in the back corner of a dingy diner in Queens, far from Sebastian's usual haunts. Three weeks had passed since the break-in, and Seth had relocated his research twice more.

"Four more victims identified." Seth kept his voice low. "All biographers or journalists. All disappeared after getting close to Sebastian though not all of them knew him by that name."

Connie nodded. "The network's been able to verify two of them. They're adding the information to the secure server."

"Network." Seth shook his head. "I still can't believe how organized you all are."

"When you lose someone to a monster, you either fall apart or you fight back." Connie's fingers traced the rim of her mug. "We chose to fight. Now that we've been acquainted for a while. I am almost ready to tell you more about why we appear so organized."

Seth thought of Emily, of the way she'd grown increasingly fascinated with Sebastian. The questions that seemed innocent but probed too deep. His stomach knotted. "I am naturally curious, but don't tell me too soon or it may compromise me. Sabastian knows too much about me and I fear it's because he can see through me."

"Well, my friends are impressed with your work." Connie leaned forward. "They'd like to meet you. Don't worry about being compromised. They have been doing this for a long while.

They are unafraid of Sabastian and what he can do. They have ways of their own, if you catch my drift."

"All right, I'll ask, then. These mysterious powerful friends you keep mentioning?" Seth raised an eyebrow. "Who are they, exactly?"

"People with resources. People who've been tracking creatures like Sebastian for generations." Connie's eyes held his. "People who can help protect you and Emily."

Seth hesitated. "What kind of people track vampires for generations?"

"The kind who've lost too much to them." Connie's voice hardened. "The kind who know how to fight back. Do you know when and how he feeds?"

No, he keeps all that extremely private. Every time I ask him about it he dismisses it as not important."

"So, he knows you are aware of what he is."

"Yeah, he knows I know."

"He doesn't want that information in the biography. If you agree to meet with my friends they can fill you in on how vampires like Sabastian feed and keep it secret."

"Okay," he said finally. "Set up the meeting."

Connie's face relaxed into a smile. "You won't regret this."

"I already regret everything about Sebastian Wolfram." Seth drained his coffee. "But at least we've kept the research safe. Small victories, right?"

"Sometimes small victories are all we get." Connie checked her watch. "I need to go. Ten-minute rule."

Seth nodded. "I'll wait five minutes before leaving."

As Connie slipped away, Seth allowed himself a moment of satisfaction. Sebastian had tried to find his research and failed. The network was growing stronger. For the first time since this nightmare began, Seth felt like he might actually survive it.

His phone buzzed with a calendar notification. The Calloway Gallery opening was tonight. Emily had been excited about it for weeks. She went on and on about a showcase of rare historical artifacts. Seth had promised to meet her there.

Seth checked his watch as he left the diner, giving Connie the agreed upon five-minute head start. The evening air carried a hint of approaching autumn, crisp enough to make him pull his jacket tighter around his shoulders. He'd need to hurry if he wanted to make it to the Calloway Gallery opening on time.

He cut through a narrow side street, his footsteps echoing between brick walls. The sound bounced back strangely as if doubled. Seth slowed, listening more carefully. The echo continued for two steps after he had stopped.

It was not an echo. It was Footsteps.

Someone was following him.

Seth's pulse quickened. He resumed walking, deliberately casual, and turned at the next corner. The footsteps continued behind him, matching his pace perfectly. He risked a glance over his shoulder but saw only shadows.

"Stay calm," he muttered to himself. "Could be nothing."

But in Sebastian's world, nothing was ever just nothing.

Seth ducked into a bodega, pretending to browse magazines while watching the street through the window. A tall figure in a dark coat paused across the street, face obscured by the gathering dusk. The stranger stood motionless, staring directly at the bodega's entrance.

"You buy or you leave," the clerk called from behind the counter.

Seth grabbed a pack of gum and paid quickly. The gallery was fifteen blocks away. Too far to run, too close for a cab to be worth the wait.

He exited the bodega and immediately turned left, walking briskly. The subway entrance loomed ahead, a potential escape route, but also a trap if his pursuer followed him below ground.

The footsteps resumed behind him, closer now. Seth's hand closed around his phone in his pocket, ready to call Emily or Connie, but who could reach him in time? What could they even do?

He took a sharp right at the next intersection, breaking into a jog. The footsteps behind him quickened in response. Seth pushed himself faster, dodging pedestrians, ignoring their irritated glances.

A cab pulled up to the curb half a block ahead, discharging passengers. Seth sprinted toward it, yanking open the door before the previous riders had fully exited.

"Calloway Gallery," he gasped, slamming the door. "Fast as you can."

The driver grunted acknowledgment and pulled into traffic. Seth twisted in his seat, scanning the sidewalk behind them. The dark figure stood at the corner, watching the cab pull away.

"Everything okay back there?" The driver eyed him in the rearview mirror.

"Fine," Seth managed. "Just running late."

The cab wove through Manhattan traffic, each block putting distance between Seth and his pursuer. He checked his phone—no messages from Emily or Connie. Nothing from Sebastian either, which somehow felt more ominous than a direct threat.

By the time the cab pulled up to the gallery, despite the quickness of the ride, Seth had almost convinced himself he'd overreacted. Almost. He paid the driver and stepped onto the sidewalk, scanning the street in both directions. No sign of the figure in the dark coat.

The gallery buzzed with Manhattan's art elite, champagne glasses clinking over conversations about provenance and artistic significance. Seth pushed through the crowd, searching for Emily's familiar form among the sea of black cocktail attire.

He spotted her near a display case containing what appeared to be ancient manuscripts. She wore a simple navy dress that made her stand out among the more ostentatious gallery patrons. Her face lit up when she saw him.

"You made it!" She kissed his cheek. "I was beginning to worry."

"Got held up." Seth glanced over his shoulder toward the entrance. "I thought someone was following me, but I think I lost them."

Emily's expression darkened. "Sebastian's people?"

"Maybe." Seth accepted a champagne flute from a passing waiter, more for something to hold than from any desire to drink. "Or just my paranoia reaching new heights."

"Your paranoia has kept you alive this long." Emily squeezed his arm. "Don't start doubting it now."

Seth nodded, allowing himself to relax slightly in her presence. Whatever, or whoever, had been following him, he'd eluded them for now. The gallery was crowded, public. Safe, at least for the moment.

"Come see this." Emily led him to the display she'd been examining. "These manuscripts are supposedly from a 15th century occult collection. The placard mentions supernatural creatures, including some that sound suspiciously like vampires."

Seth leaned closer to the glass case, examining the faded script. The familiar knot of tension returned to his stomach. Even here, surrounded by New York's elite, Sebastian's shadow seemed to follow him.

"I am going to find the restroom. I need to splash some water on my face."

"Are you sure you're all right? Emily asked with concern in her voice.

"Of course, I'll be right back."

He left Emily for only a few moments, just enough to splash some cold water on his face and use the facilities. When he returned to the festivities, he couldn't find her at first. He looked for her where he left her, and she wasn't anywhere near.

He finally spotted her near a display of medieval artwork, champagne flute in hand. But she wasn't alone.

Sebastian stood beside her, impeccable in a tailored black suit. He leaned close, whispering something that made Emily laugh. His hand rested on the small of her back, possessive and intimate.

Seth's blood ran cold. Emily tilted her head up toward Sebastian, her expression rapt with attention. The same expression Seth had seen drawn in pencil on countless faces in Winston's journal. He recognized it as the look of someone falling under Sebastian's spell.

The champagne flute in Seth's hand threatened to shatter in his grip. Sebastian's eyes lifted, meeting Seth's across the room. A smile spread across the vampire's face. It was not the polished, public smile he wore for others, but something predatory and triumphant.

The message was clear. Sebastian had found Seth's weakness and was exploiting it ruthlessly. He wasn't just trying to seduce Emily, he was taking her, deliberately. Seth's fears had come true. Pike's warning echoed in his head. *He is waiting to find out who he can use against you!*

Chapter 10
The Dark Purpose of Evil

Seth stood frozen in place, watching as Sebastian bent to whisper something else in Emily's ear. Her laugh floated across the gallery, the sound twisting in his gut like a knife.

Seth's phone vibrated in his pocket. He pulled it out with trembling fingers, grateful for the distraction. A text from Connie: "Coffee shop on 9th. Now."

He typed back; I can't right now.

His phone vibrated again. It's not negotiable.

He glanced back at Emily and Sebastian. Neither had noticed him yet, or at least, Emily hadn't. Sebastian's eyes flicked toward him again, that predatory smile widening slightly before returning his full attention to Emily.

Seth backed away, slipping through the crowd toward the exit. Every instinct compelled him to confront them, to drag

Emily away, but he knew better. A public scene would only play into Sebastian's hands.

The night air hit him like a slap as he burst onto the sidewalk. He hailed a cab. Sebastian had found his weakness. He had planned it from the beginning. This wasn't a chance encounter. This was calculated as Nathan Pike had warned him.

Twenty minutes later, Seth slid into a booth across from Connie. The coffee shop was nearly empty, just a barista wiping down counters and an elderly man reading a newspaper.

"He's got Emily," Seth blurted out, his voice shaky. "I saw them together at the gallery. She looked like she was completely enamored with him."

Connie's face tightened. "I was afraid of this. How long were they talking?"

"I don't know. I left her for five minutes, maybe less. He was touching her, whispering to her, and she was laughing."

"Classic technique." Connie's voice was grim. "He's isolating you, taking away your support system."

"I need to know how to stop him." Seth leaned forward, desperation clawing at his throat. "You said your friends could help. Whatever they know, whatever they can do, I'm ready."

Connie studied him for a long moment, then nodded. "I've set up the meeting. Tonight."

"Where?"

"It's not public, so we don't need to worry about the ten-minute rule. You can talk as long as necessary." She wrote an address on a napkin. "Go there in an hour."

Seth pocketed the address. "What is this place?"

"The Rose and Raven Society." Connie's voice dropped to just above a whisper. "They've been tracking creatures like Sebastian for centuries. If anyone can help you, it's them."

"A secret society?" Seth couldn't keep the skepticism from his voice.

"You're dealing with a vampire, Seth. Did you expect the solution to come from the NYPD? The Rose and Raven Society has documented every supernatural encounter on record since the early 1800s. They know Sebastian's patterns better than anyone."

Seth nodded, too exhausted to argue. "I'll go. But what about Emily?"

"Don't contact her. Not yet." Connie's expression softened. "If Sebastian has begun his influence, anything you say will get back to him. Let the Society advise you first."

"Is she lost?" He was almost afraid to hear the answer.

Connie nodded, "She's glamoured. She is lost for now."

"For now? There's a chance?"

"There's always a chance, but don't hold out hope. Once a vampire like Sabastian works his magic, it's tough to overcome."

An hour later, Seth stood before an unmarked door in a renovated warehouse district. The building looked ordinary enough, with a brick facade, clean windows, discreet security cameras. Nothing to suggest it housed a centuries-old secret society dedicated to supernatural investigation.

He pressed the intercom button. A crisp voice answered: "Yes?"

"Connie Stone sent me. I have a meeting scheduled."

A pause, then the door buzzed open. Seth stepped into a lobby that could have belonged to any upscale firm complete with polished floors, tasteful artwork, and subdued lighting. A woman in a blue dress approached him.

"Mr. Aubrey?"

"Yes."

"This way, please."

She led him through a maze of corridors to a wood-paneled library that seemed transplanted from another century. Floor-to-ceiling bookshelves lined the walls, leather-bound volumes organized with meticulous care. A man rose from behind an antique desk as they entered.

"Seth Aubrey." The man extended his hand. "Henry Higgins, I run this place. Connie has told me about your situation."

Seth shook his hand, noting the firm grip and sharp, assessing eyes. "She said you might be able to help me understand what I'm dealing with."

"We've been tracking Sebastian Wolfram for a very long time." Higgins gestured to a chair. "Please, sit. We have much to discuss."

Seth sank into the offered seat, suddenly aware of how exhausted he felt. "He's got Emily. My... friend."

"Yes, Connie mentioned that." Higgins sat across from him. "We have people at the gallery now. They will do whatever they can to help. You must realize, though, that she may already be too far gone. This bastard works quickly."

"I appreciate any help."

Higgins reassured him with a single nod, "Now, getting to the other thing. Sebastian's methodology is quite consistent. He selects writers not just for their skill, but for their vulnerabilities."

"What do you mean?"

"Sebastian doesn't just feed on blood, Mr. Aubrey. He feeds on despair." Higgins leaned forward. "He chooses writers who are already predisposed to self-destruction, that is to say people with relationship problems, financial troubles, ethical conflicts. Then he amplifies those tendencies, pushing them toward ruin. Connie told me of your suspicions, and you are correct. Sabastian feeds off human suffering and despair as well as blood. His method of feeding minimizes his need to take in blood, which means he can coexist with us humans for much longer without anyone suspecting. But, in order to be successful at it, he must always have someone like you on the metaphorical leash. "

Seth thought of his breakup with Faith, his financial struggles, the moral compromises he'd made for his career. "He's been setting me up from the beginning."

"Precisely." Higgins nodded. "The biography is merely a pretext. He never intends for it to be completed. The real purpose is to draw you in, isolate you, and then watch as you destroy yourself."

Seth spoke, his voice hoarse. "So, he does it to feed so he doesn't have to hunt for human blood?"

"Yes, but he does have to hunt for blood eventually, just not as often." Connie's voice came from the doorway as she entered the room. "Emotional sustenance is what he gains from it. Vampires like Sebastian feed on more than just blood. They feed on human suffering, particularly the suffering of creative minds."

"That's what Higgins was just explaining to me." Seth felt sick.

"He will only feed off it in person. There is no mental connection as some believe. I assume he requires daily briefings in person?" Higgins asked.

"Yes, he does." Seth said. "Although for the past month or so I have not been around him. I ran."

"So, Connie has told me. That's probably why he has appeared at the gallery. He is tracking Emily to get to you."

Higgins pulled a leather-bound book from his desk. "We've documented fifty-seven cases over the last century alone. The pattern is always the same: commission a biography, manipulate the writer into isolation and paranoia, then watch as they unravel, often taking loved ones down with them."

Seth leaned forward, his fingers digging into the armrests of the chair. The impact of what Higgins and Connie were telling him hit him hard. It all made sense now, Sebastian's careful manipulation, the way he'd isolated Seth, the strategic targeting of Emily.

"So he's not just after my biography," Seth said, his voice steadier than he felt. "He's feeding on my misery."

"Precisely." Higgins nodded, his expression grave. "The biography is merely the hook. Your suffering is the meal."

Seth thought of Emily's face at the gallery, that rapt expression as Sebastian whispered in her ear. His chest tightened with a mixture of fear and rage.

"I believe you," Seth said. "Everything you're saying matches what I've seen, what I've experienced. Sebastian is exactly the kind of vampire you're describing." He took a deep breath. "So now I need to know how to stop him. How to defeat him permanently. And how to help Emily, if I still can."

Higgins exchanged a glance with Connie. "Defeating a vampire like Sebastian isn't simple, Mr. Aubrey. He's survived for centuries by being cautious, strategic."

"I don't care how difficult it is," Seth insisted. "He has Emily. He's destroyed countless lives. Tell me what I need to do."

Higgins opened a drawer in his desk and removed a massive, ancient leather-bound tome. "Traditional methods like stakes, sunlight, and holy water, will have varying degrees of effectiveness depending on the vampire's age and lineage, but you might need more."

"Sunlight won't do it. Sebastian moves around during daylight," Seth pointed out. "I've seen him."

"The older they get, the more they can tolerate," Connie explained. "Sunlight weakens him, but it won't destroy him outright unless he's exposed for extended periods."

"He doesn't seem to be affected by it at all." Seth said.

"He has moved past it." Connie said.

Higgins nodded. "The most reliable method for him then is probably decapitation, followed by burning the remains. But getting close enough to accomplish that..." He trailed off meaningfully.

Seth swallowed hard. The clinical discussion of beheading someone, even a monster like Sebastian, made his stomach turn.

"What about Emily? How do I break his hold on her? That is, assuming she is as far gone as you both have indicated."

"Again, there is no way to know exactly how far gone she is. If she has a strong will, you might be able to break her free from it fairly easily. If he really wants her, I mean he is attracted to her and really wants her as his own and not merely to destroy you, his glamour will be stronger. It depends on how far his influence has progressed," Connie said. "In the early stages, simply separating them might be enough. But once he feeds on her..."

"Feeds on her?" Seth's voice rose. "You mean he will feed on her?"

"Not for blood necessarily," Higgins interjected. "Vampires like Sebastian often begin with emotional feeding, by drawing out fear, desire, and fascination. It creates a bond that makes the eventual blood-taking more... satisfying for them."

Seth felt sick. "How do I know what stage she's in?"

"Changes in behavior," Connie said. "Unusual fascination with him, defending him, making excuses to see him. Later stages include physical symptoms like pallor, fatigue, and unexplained marks or bruises."

Seth thought back to Emily's questions about Sebastian, her growing curiosity about his appearance, his voice. Had that been the beginning of his influence? Or just natural interest in the subject of Seth's work?

"I need to get her away from him," Seth said firmly. "I must go to her."

"Not without preparation," Higgins warned. "If you confront Sebastian directly, you'll likely end up dead, and Emily will still remain in his thrall."

"Then what do I do?" Seth demanded, frustration building. "I can't just leave her with him!"

Higgins opened the ancient journal, turning to a marked page. "There are ways to weaken him first. Vampires of Sebastian's lineage have specific vulnerabilities. Their power comes from blood, yes, but also from their possessions, items they've carried through the centuries."

"Like what?"

"Personal artifacts. Things that connect them to their human past." Higgins turned the journal so Seth could see the handwritten notes. "Destroy these, and you diminish their power."

Seth remembered the wooden box in Sebastian's library—the one containing Elsa Brenner's letters and daguerreotype. The way Sebastian had snatched it away when Seth showed too much interest.

"I think I know what some of those might be," Seth said slowly. "But they're in his penthouse. He hovers around them."

"We can help with that," Connie said. "The Society has resources. We have people trained to deal with these situations."

"As far as you are concerned, and if you want to break the vampire's hold in Emily, I have something here in this book, that might aid you."

"What? I will do anything."

"There are rituals," Higgins said carefully. "Old methods of severing vampiric bonds. But they're dangerous, especially if the connection has deepened."

Seth nodded, "Tell me everything. Whatever it takes, I'll do it."

Higgins studied him for a long moment, then nodded. "Very well. But understand this, Mr. Aubrey, once you move against Sebastian, there's no going back. He will know, and he will retaliate with everything he has."

"I understand," Seth said, his voice firm despite the fear churning in his gut. "I'm already dead to him anyway. The moment I stopped being his obedient biographer, I became expendable."

"These rituals will change you, probably forever." Higgins cautioned. "You should not enter into an agreement with us to undergo the rituals unless you are one hundred percent certain."

"Understood, what do I need to do?"

Chapter 11
Stranglehold

Seth stepped out of the Rose and Raven Society headquarters, the night air cool against his face. His mind buzzed with everything Higgins had told him. He was considering the rituals, no matter how dangerous they may be, but Higgins insisted he think hard on it first. He gave him a few hours to mull over the decision. For the first time since this nightmare began, he had a plan. Not just to survive, but to fight back. He was determined to rid himself of the fear and face the vampire on the equal footing Higgins was offering him. Emily had been the catalyst that took him from frightened victim to...something else.

The subway ride to Sebastian's penthouse felt surreal. Around him, New Yorkers scrolled through phones, dozed against windows, lived their normal lives. None of them knew about the predator in their midst, the centuries of blood and manipulation. Hell, there might even be more monsters among them, perhaps even riding on the very train they were riding on right now.

Seth clutched his messenger bag containing the latest biography chapters. The pages were bait, a reason to enter the lion's den while he assessed potential weaknesses. He'd memorized Higgins' instructions: locate the artifacts, identify security vulnerabilities, maintain the facade of cooperation.

The elevator ascended to Sebastian's penthouse with stomach-dropping speed. Seth used those moments to compose his features, to bury his newfound knowledge beneath a mask of professional detachment.

"Ah, Seth." Sebastian materialized from the shadows as the elevator doors opened. "Have you come to the decision to return to me?"

"What are you talking about? I never left you. I simply needed time and a place to write. What did you expect? Did you think the pages would just materialize?"

"Hmm, you are different. You are no longer trying to keep your expressions and words neutral for my benefit."

"I have no idea what you mean." He held out the folder containing the pages. "Are you going to take this?"

Sebastian accepted the folder and opened it. He examined the pages and flipped through them, his expression unreadable. "Your writing has improved. Less... emotional than your previous work."

"I'm trying to maintain objectivity." Seth moved toward the study, where they usually conducted their meetings.

"Are you?" Sebastian closed the folder. "Even after I've taken Emily from you?"

Seth's step faltered, but he recovered quickly. "What do you mean, taken?"

Sebastian's smile changed into a confused grin. "Come now, Seth. Let's not play games. I've been planning this since you first met her at that quaint little coffee shop."

Ice spread through Seth's veins. Sebastian had been watching him even then, before the biography, before any of this began. He forced his expression to remain the same, remembering Higgins' warning: vampires like Sabastian feed on emotional suffering. "You are mistaken. She means nothing to me. How can you take someone from me I never possessed?"

"I know you have been intimate. You are hurting inside, suffering."

"Nope, I'm really not. Emily's free to make her own choices." Seth shrugged, the gesture requiring every ounce of his acting ability.

Sebastian circled him slowly, predator assessing prey. "Impressive. You're trying very hard to hide your anguish. But I can feel it, Seth. The hurt radiating from you at the thought of losing her to me."

Seth met his gaze steadily. "The biography is my priority. My personal life is separate."

"Is it?" Sebastian's voice dropped to a silky whisper. "Then you won't mind if I prove my point."

He snapped his fingers, the sound unnaturally sharp in the vast penthouse. Footsteps echoed from the hallway, and Seth's heart contracted painfully as Emily appeared. He held all his feelings inside. He forced them down.

She looked different somehow, her skin paler, her movements more fluid. She wore an elegant black dress he'd never seen before, her hair styled in a way that emphasized the graceful curve of her neck.

"Seth," she began, "Sebastian said you'd be stopping by."

Seth fought to keep his breathing even. "Emily. I didn't expect to see you here."

"I have exciting news." She moved to Sebastian's side, her body language intimate, familiar. "I'm taking a sabbatical from the Times. Sebastian's invited me to join him in Europe for his research."

"Has he? Europe huh, sounds stimulating." Seth allowed the sarcasm in his voice, understanding the full scope of Sebastian's game. This was the next phase. He was not just taking Emily but flaunting it. He was forcing Seth to witness his triumph.

"Venice, Prague, Vienna." Sebastian's hand settled possessively on Emily's waist. "All the places I've described in our sessions. Emily will help document the journey."

Seth recognized the trap. Sebastian wanted his pain, his jealousy, his desperation. The vampire fed on those emotions as surely as he fed on blood. With supreme effort, Seth manufactured a smile.

"Sounds like an *amazing* opportunity. The European chapters needed firsthand research."

Sebastian's eyes narrowed slightly, the only indication that Seth's reaction wasn't what he'd expected.

"You're not... concerned?" Emily asked, a flicker of her old self showing through whatever hold Sebastian had on her.

"Why would I be?" Seth maintained his casual tone. "It's a professional arrangement. The biography will benefit from your perspective."

Sebastian's fingers tightened on Emily's waist. "Perhaps Seth doesn't care for you as deeply as you thought, my dear."

Seth caught the flash of hurt in Emily's eyes and nearly broke character. He wanted to grab her, shake her, make her see what was happening. Instead, he checked his watch.

"When do you leave?"

"Tomorrow evening," Sebastian answered, his voice carrying an edge of frustration. "A private flight from Teterboro."

"I should get those notes to you before you go, then." Seth directed this to Emily, searching her face for any sign of the woman he knew.

Sebastian stepped between them, his movement too fast for a human. "That won't be necessary. Emily and I have everything we need."

The air in the room seemed to thicken. Sebastian's eyes locked with Seth's, pupils expanding until they swallowed the iris entirely. Seth felt a pressure building in his mind, like hands trying to pry open a locked door.

"You will continue your work here," Sebastian said, his voice resonating with unnatural power. "Alone. Without interference."

Seth's vision tunneled, the edges darkening as Sebastian's will pressed against his consciousness. This was glamour. The vampire's ability to dominate human minds. Seth hadn't believed it possible until this moment, feeling his thoughts being reshaped by Sebastian's influence. He fought it.

With monumental effort, Seth maintained eye contact, pretending to submit while mentally recoiling. The pressure receded slightly.

"Of course," Seth said, his voice deliberately flat. "I'll focus on the biography."

Sebastian smiled, satisfied with his apparent victory. "Excellent. We'll be in touch from Europe."

Seth's jaw clenched as he watched Sebastian's hand slide possessively around Emily's waist. The vampire's fingers pressed tightly against the black fabric of her dress, pale against the dark material. Each second of contact sent fresh waves of rage through Seth's body, despite his best efforts to appear unmoved.

"The itinerary is quite extensive," Sebastian continued, his eyes never leaving Seth's face. "Emily will document locations significant to my past. Vienna's opera house, where I first heard Mozart perform. The palazzo in Venice where I witnessed the fall of the republic."

Emily nodded, her expression rapt with fascination. "Sebastian's firsthand accounts will add authenticity the biography has been lacking."

The subtle dig pierced Seth's composure. His fingers curled into his palms, nails biting into flesh. The pain helped him focus, helped him fight against the glamour still pressing at the edges of his mind.

"I'm sure they will," Seth managed, his voice tight despite his efforts.

Sebastian's lips curved upward, satisfaction flickering across his features. He'd noticed the crack in Seth's facade, the slight tremor in his voice, the tension in his shoulders. The vampire was feeding on these small betrayals of emotion, drawing sustenance from Seth's poorly concealed pain.

"Emily has such a... fresh perspective," Sebastian murmured, "Her questions are most illuminating."

Seth watched Emily lean into Sebastian's touch, her eyes half-closed with pleasure. This wasn't the sharp, skeptical journalist who had challenged Seth's ethics and pushed him to reclaim his investigative instincts. This was someone else, someone under Sebastian's thrall.

"I'm glad you've found a suitable research assistant," Seth said, the words tasting like ash in his mouth.

Sebastian's smile widened fractionally. "Oh, she's much more than that."

The vampire bent his head toward Emily, his lips brushing against her ear as he whispered something that made her cheeks flush. Seth's vision blurred red at the edges. His composure faltered in his mind as rage threatened to overwhelm his concentration.

"Seth?" Emily's voice cut through his fury. "Are you feeling all right? You look flushed."

"I'm fine." The words came out harsher than he intended. Another slip, another morsel of emotion for Sebastian to devour.

"Perhaps you should sit down." Sebastian gestured toward the leather armchair, false concern dripping from his voice. "You seem... distressed."

Seth remained standing, forcing his breathing to steady. "Just tired. Deadline pressure."

"Of course." Sebastian's knowing smile made it clear he saw through the lie. "The biography remains your priority, as you said."

Emily stepped away from Sebastian, approaching Seth with a frown creasing her forehead. For a moment, she looked like herself again, concerned, perceptive, present.

"Seth, if this arrangement is uncomfortable for you—"

"It's not," Seth interrupted, too quickly. Another crack in his performance.

Sebastian appeared at Emily's side with unnatural speed, his hand settling on her shoulder. "Seth understands professional boundaries, don't you, Seth?"

The question carried a double edge, a reminder of Seth's supposed commitment to the biography, and a taunt about the personal boundaries Sebastian was deliberately violating.

Seth's teeth ground together as he fought to maintain control. The glamour pressed harder against his mind, seeking entry through the cracks in his emotional armor. Sebastian was using his anger, his jealousy, to weaken his mental defenses.

"Perfectly," Seth replied, forcing his features into a neutral expression. "I should go to let you both prepare for your trip."

Sebastian did not seem to like his words, disappointment flashing across his features. He'd been hoping for more. Perhaps he was hoping for a confrontation, an emotional outburst, something to feast upon.

"So soon?" The vampire's voice carried a hint of frustration. "I thought we might discuss the chapters you've brought. There are several... inaccuracies that need addressing."

"Another time." Seth moved toward the elevator, needing to escape before his control shattered completely. He remembered the vampire had not that read much of the pages he brought. "You have packing to do."

Emily looked between them, confusion coloring her expression. "Seth—"

"Have a good trip, Emily." Seth cut her off, unable to bear hearing her voice, seeing her under Sebastian's influence. "Send postcards."

Sebastian's lips thinned with displeasure. He'd expected more resistance, more emotional turmoil to feed upon. Seth's retreat, while not entirely convincing, was denying him the full meal he'd anticipated.

"We'll be in touch," Sebastian called as the elevator doors closed. "I'm sure you'll have plenty to occupy yourself with while we're away."

The threat beneath the casual words was unmistakable. The elevator began it's descent. Only then did he allow his composure to crack, his hands shaking as he pressed them against the cool metal walls. he collapsed against the rear of the elevator.

Chapter 12
Time to Think

Seth stumbled into his apartment, the encounter with Sebastian and Emily still burning in his mind. He slammed the door behind him, leaning against it as if to physically hold back the horror of what he'd witnessed. Emily's vacant eyes, her body language, the way she leaned into Sebastian's touch. It was all wrong, all twisted.

He pushed himself away from the door and paced the small living room. The choice before him became brutally clear: he was going to fight back against a creature who had centuries of experience destroying those who opposed him and win somehow. He was determined to win in any way he could, even if that meant letting Higgins perform his ritual.

"Screw it," Seth muttered, grabbing his jacket again. "I'm not letting him take her."

An hour later, he sat across from Henry Higgins in the wood-paneled library of the Rose and Raven Society. The older man's face remained impassive as Seth recounted his encounter with Sebastian and Emily.

"He's taking her to Europe tomorrow. Private flight from Teterboro." His words came out all in rapid succession. "I couldn't even reach her. It's like she's there, but not there."

Higgins nodded gravely. "The glamour is powerful, especially in the early stages. She's still fighting it, even if she doesn't realize it."

"You mentioned a ritual and you gave me time to consider it. I've considered it and I want you to do it. Give me the ability to meet Sabastian on his level of power and influence!"

"There are methods." Higgins steepled his fingers. "But first, we need to discuss your latent talents, Mr. Aubrey. Then we can use the ritual to augment them."

Seth frowned. "My latent talents?"

"You've shown remarkable resistance to Sebastian's influence. Most humans succumb completely to a vampire of his age and power." Higgins looked him directly in the eye. "Have you ever experienced anything... unusual? Moments of inexplicable intuition? Strange dreams?"

"What does this have to do with my latent talents and saving Emily?"

"Everything." Higgins rose and moved to a locked cabinet. "Every human possesses latent paranormal abilities. Most remain dormant throughout their lives, suppressed by societal conditioning and biological safeguards. Humans can actually do anything they can think of, but there is something in our brains that says no, you can't and that's what holds us back. Remove that barrier, and your latent talents, the ones that come through regardless of your brain telling you no, are the strongest."

Seth watched as Higgins removed an ancient-looking box from the cabinet. "You're saying I have... what? Psychic powers?"

"I'm saying you have potential." Higgins set the box on the desk between them. "We can perform a ritual that would unlock those mental blocks, reveal your true capabilities. It might give you the edge you need against Sebastian."

Seth stared at the box, skepticism warring with desperation. "Is it dangerous?"

"All power comes with risk." Higgins' expression remained neutral. "The choice is yours."

"I'll risk it if it will put me in the position to take down Sabastian."

"It might and it might not. We don't control the outcome of the ritual. I need time to prepare. I'll text you when I'm ready for you to return here. Are you certain you want to try this?"

"Yes. Make your preparations. I will await your text."

Back in his apartment, Seth opened his laptop and created two new document folders: "Authorized" and "True." His fingers lingered over the keyboard as he gathered together his thoughts, then he began to write feverishly. The words came flowing out of his head as he crafted two parallel narratives. The first one was the sanitized version Sebastian expected, and the true account of the vampire's centuries of manipulation and murder was the second.

His phone buzzed with a text. He got excited until he saw it was from Emily: "Don't bother with those next few chapters. Sebastian says your services won't be needed much longer."

The cold dismissal sent a chill through Seth's body. This wasn't Emily, not the woman who had challenged him to reclaim his journalistic integrity, who had looked at him with warmth and understanding. This was Sebastian's puppet, her words shaped by his influence.

Seth typed back: "Tell Sebastian I'm making excellent progress. The biography will be everything he wants."

Let the vampire think he was still the obedient biographer, still playing by Sebastian's rules. It would buy him time.

Three days later, Emily called. Seth hoped that somehow she'd broken free of Sebastian's control and thought to call him to come pick her up. It was wishful thinking. .

"Emily? Are you okay?"

"I'm calling about your apartment." Her voice was flat, emotionless. "I need to pick up some research materials Sebastian wants."

"Emily, listen to me. This isn't you. Sebastian is—"

"Don't be pathetic, Seth." The cruelty in her tone sliced through him. "Sebastian showed me what you really are. You're just a hack writer who destroys reputations for money. Did you really think I would care about you enough to get passed that?"

Seth's grip tightened on the phone. "That's Sebastian talking, not you."

"I'll be there at three to collect the materials." She hung up without another word.

Seth stared at the silent phone, grief and rage swelling within him. In that moment, his decision was made once and for all, beyond any doubt. He would expose Sebastian, whatever the personal cost. He would save Emily, even if she hated him for it. He would end this centuries-long cycle of manipulation and destruction.

He dialed Higgins' number. "How are the preparations going? I know you said wait for your text, but when can we do the ritual?"

"I am ready when you are. If I doubted your conviction, I don't anymore. You really do want this."

"Yes, I do."

"Alright, get over here." Higgins said then hung up.

The preparation room at the Rose and Raven Society was unlike anything Seth had imagined. He expected it to be clinical, but instead it was inviting. It was a skylit room with polished wood and spectacular marble. Symbols he didn't recognize were etched into the floor and walls. Equipment that looked part medical, part mystical surrounded a central table.

"The procedure will be uncomfortable," Higgins explained as assistants prepared various instruments. "Your mind has built defenses over decades. Breaking through them requires... intensity."

Seth lay on the table. "I trust you as long as this will give me the ability to defeat Sabastian."

"It will give you the tools." Higgins placed a hand on Seth's shoulder. "The rest depends on how you use them."

As they secured restraints around his wrists and ankles, Seth realized he was about to cross a threshold from which there was no return. But the image of Emily's vacant eyes, her cruel words, steeled his resolve.

"I'm ready," he said.

The first wave of pain crashed through him like electricity, his back arching off the table as ancient words filled the room. Seth screamed as barriers in his mind began to dissolve, revealing glimpses of something vast and terrifying beyond. It was all so simple, terrifying, but simple.

Chapter 13
Ancient Knowledge

Seth's body convulsed as the ritual reached its crescendo. The pain receded like a tide, leaving behind something new, a clarity that sharpened his senses to knife-edge precision. When he opened his eyes, the world looked different. Colors seemed more vivid, sounds more distinct. The members of the Rose and Raven Society watched him with expressions ranging from curiosity to awe.

"How do you feel?" Higgins asked, helping Seth sit up.

"Different." Seth flexed his fingers, noting how each movement seemed more deliberate, more controlled. "What happened?"

"The ritual worked." Higgins' voice carried a note of surprise. "Better than expected, actually. Your natural resistance to glamour has been amplified, among other things yet to be revealed."

Seth swung his legs over the edge of the table, testing his balance. "Amplified how?"

"We won't know the full extent until you face Sebastian again." Higgins handed him a glass of water. "But based on the readings, you should be completely immune to his influence now."

"What other things will be revealed?"

"If I knew, I'd tell you. Most people who go through the ritual gain psychic gifts unknown to us until they manifest. Some gain a sense of the unknown, some can break down barriers in other people's minds, some can even reverse the influence of glamouring, but I don't want you to get your hopes up. You may not be able to free Emily of Sabastian's influence."

Seth drank deeply, the water tasting sweeter than he remembered. "So, I might be able to save Emily. Will I be able to face him one on one?"

"It's a start." Higgins checked Seth's pupils, nodding with satisfaction. "You need to give it a few days for your mind to adjust. There may be still other abilities that manifest we have not yet discovered or even know about. The ritual unlocks potential, and what form that takes depends on the individual. We use this ritual on all society agents on a voluntary basis and sometimes nothing happens."

"You mean I may see something happen besides the glamour resistance and whatnot?"

"Yes, or as I said, you may see nothing further manifest. It's always somewhat of a mystery as to how the individual mind will react."

"Thanks, Higgins."

"My pleasure. Now, I would say go rest for at least three days then report back to me.

"Three days, got it!"

Three days later, Seth stood in his apartment, waiting for Emily's arrival. He'd prepared carefully, setting up subtle protections Higgins had provided, nothing obvious enough to alert Sebastian, but enough to give Seth an edge if things went wrong.

The knock came precisely at three. Seth opened the door to find Emily standing there, her face a mask of cold indifference. Behind her, a tall figure lingered in the hallway shadows. It had to be Sebastian, watching from a distance.

"The research materials," Emily said flatly, extending her hand.

Seth stepped back, allowing her to enter. "Come in. I'll get them for you."

As Emily crossed the threshold, Seth felt a pressure against his mind. Sebastian was attempting to extend his influence through Emily. The sensation was like fingers probing at a locked door, searching for weaknesses. He could feel what the vampire was trying to do, a new ability for him.

Seth also noticed where before such attempts by Sabastian to test his resolve had required all his concentration to resist, now he felt only a mild discomfort. The ritual had worked, he could easily seal his mind against Sebastian's intrusions. The vampire must be reeling from frustration.

"Sebastian's with you, isn't he?" Seth asked, moving to his desk where he'd prepared a folder of carefully selected materials.

Emily's expression didn't change. "He's concerned you might try something foolish."

"Like what?" Seth handed her the folder, deliberately brushing his fingers against hers to see if the contact gave him any insight. It didn't. "Trying to save you from a monster?"

A flicker of something, recognition, perhaps, crossed Emily's face before the blank mask returned. "I don't need saving."

"He's feeding on you, Emily." Seth kept his voice low. "Maybe not blood, but certainly your emotions, your will. He's hollowing you out."

Emily's lips curled into a sneer. "You're pathetic. Jealous because I chose him over you."

The words stung, but Seth recognized them as Sebastian's, not Emily's. He felt the vampire's satisfaction radiating through the vampire's connection with her.

Something shifted in Seth's awareness. He could feel Sebastian's hunger, his anticipation of Seth's suffering, and with that awareness came an instinctive understanding. What would Sabastian do if he was anticipating pain and suffering through Emily's rejections like usual from him and Seth denied him for the first time?

Seth closed his eyes, focusing on the pain Emily's words had caused. Instead of fighting it or suppressing it, he transformed it, reshaping the hurt into something else. Joy. Contentment. Satisfaction.

The effect was immediate. Through the connection, Seth felt Sebastian recoil, as if tasting something bitter when expecting sweetness.

Emily blinked, momentarily breaking through her trance. "What are you doing?"

Seth stepped closer, maintaining his focus on positive emotions. "Fighting back."

He reached for Emily's hand again, this time holding it firmly. Sebastian's glamour surrounded her like a dark aura, visible to Seth's newly enhanced perception, another manifested ability he wasn't expecting. He could see how it worked. Dark tendrils of influence ran from the aura around Emily connecting back to Sebastian himself.

Seth concentrated, reflecting the glamour back along those connections. Not just resisting but reversing the flow. The technique came to him instinctively, as if he'd always known how to do it but had forgotten until this moment.

Through their linked hands, Seth felt Emily's confusion deepen as Sebastian's hold weakened. In the hallway, the vampire hissed, a sound no human throat could make.

"He can't control you if you don't let him," Seth whispered, pouring his newfound ability into breaking Sebastian's grip on Emily's mind.

For a brief, shining moment, recognition flared in Emily's eyes, and her true self came fighting to the surface.

"Seth?" Her voice wavered, the flat affect giving way to confusion. "What's happening to me?"

Seth opened his mouth to answer, but before the words came, a force like an invisible battering ram slammed into him, breaking his connection with Emily. He staggered backward, his shoulders hitting the wall as Sebastian materialized in the doorway. The vampire's face was contorted with rage, his usual smooth facade gone to reveal something ancient and monstrous beneath.

"What have you done?" Sebastian hissed, his voice resonating with unnatural harmonics.

Emily clutched her head, swaying unsteadily. "Sebastian? I feel... strange."

Seth pushed himself off the wall, keeping his eyes locked on Sebastian. The vampire's aura pulsed with dark energy, visible now to him. Tendrils of that darkness still connected to Emily, though noticeably weakened where Seth had disrupted them. Seth cursed he was not yet experienced enough with his abilities to take him on completely. Sabastian was still too strong for him.

"You're stronger than you should be," Sebastian snarled, circling toward Seth with predatory grace. "Someone has been interfering."

"I don't know what you mean." Seth blurted out. "I'm the same as I've always been.

"No, you're not." Sebastian said slowly as he made deliberate eye contact with Seth. "Something about you is very, very different." His eyes narrowed to slits. "What have they done to you, Seth? What foolish ritual have you undergone? You realize they use tactics as unsavory as you believe I do."

"Who's they?" Seth replied.

He felt Sebastian's mind press against his, probing for weaknesses. Unlike before, the pressure felt distant, manageable, like hearing someone shouting from behind thick glass. The ritual had worked even better than Higgins had suggested. "It won't work, Sabastian. Already I can feel my resistance to your ways strengthening. What's different about me is that I know you. That knowledge is power, and I can use it to resist you."

"Leave him alone," Emily said, her voice stronger now. She took a hesitant step toward Seth, then winced as Sebastian's influence tightened around her again.

"Emily," Sebastian said, his voice dropping to a hypnotic cadence. "Wait in the hallway. Our business here is concluded."

Emily's face went slack again. She turned toward the door without saying another word, the folder clutched to her chest.

"No!" Seth lunged forward, but Sebastian moved with inhuman speed, placing himself between Seth and Emily.

"You've surprised me, Seth. Few have managed that in the past four centuries." Sebastian's lips curled into something resembling a smile. "But your little parlor trick changes nothing. Emily is mine now."

"She's not property," Seth growled. "And whatever you've done to her, I can undo it."

"Can you?" Sebastian's voice was silky, dangerous. "I've had her blood, Seth. We're connected in ways you can't comprehend."

The admission sent ice through Seth's veins. Sebastian had already begun feeding on Emily, not just emotionally, but physically. The transformation was further along than he'd feared. "Spoken like a true melodramatic fiend from a ninetieth century dime novel. You're pathetic, Sabastian."

"That may be, but your insult changes nothing. She is bent to my will."

"She's fighting you," Seth said, focusing his newfound abilities to sense the connection between them. "I can feel it."

Sebastian's aura flickered with irritation. "A temporary inconvenience. By the time we reach Vienna, her resistance, and everything you are trying to do here, will be entirely gone. You may be stronger than before, but you are still laughably weak compared to me. All you have have done is remind me how much I have slacked off. I will work on that weakness now."

"Vienna?" Seth latched onto the information. "You're still leaving tomorrow?"

"Change of plans." Sebastian smiled coldly. "We depart tonight. Your little awakening has accelerated my timetable." He glanced toward the door. "Emily has been most helpful in explaining your research methods. We know all about your contact with Nathan, your hidden notes, your growing suspicions."

Seth gnashed his teeth. Emily had betrayed his methods to Sebastian while under his influence. Everything Seth had worked to hide had been compromised.

"What do you want from her?" Seth demanded. "You've had countless writers, countless biographers. Why Emily?"

"Because she was once yours. Because she matters to you," Sebastian replied simply. "And because she possesses something I need for what comes next."

"What comes next?" Seth repeated, he dared not hope the vampire would actually tell him.

"The Chronicler's Ascension," Sebastian said, watching Seth's face closely for recognition. Finding none, he continued, "Of course, they wouldn't have told you everything. The Rose and Raven Society guards its secrets well, even from its own pawns."

"The Rose and who now? What the hell are you talking about?"

"You wreak of them. I will destroy them and you."

There it was. Sabastian couldn't help himself. Perhaps an older vampire could guard his secrets better. He decided to press him further while still trying to reach Emily.

"Tell me," Seth said, stalling for time as he tried to strengthen his connection to Emily while she was still visible through the open doorway. "How do you plan to do that?"

Sebastian laughed, the sound devoid of humor. "You think me a villain from one of your modern films, eager to monologue about my plans?" He stepped closer, his eyes boring into Seth's. "You are my seventh biographer, Seth. The final piece in a puzzle I've been assembling for over a century."

"Seventh?" Seth repeated, "centuries? But I thought you were turned during World War II. Isn't that what you told me? Oh, that was before you told me about all that stuff that happened to you much earlier. Tell me, does anyone believe your lies or are they just told to your biographers to keep them off balance so you can feed off their confusion. He began connecting fragments of information from Winston's journal, from Connie, from the Society's archives. "Morrison, Chenowith... the others. All lies to keep them in your web."

He lingered on the question of his origin with a sly grin before he answered. "Each served their purpose, as will you." Sebastian glanced at his watch, an incongruously human gesture. "But I've indulged this conversation long enough. Emily and I have a plane to catch."

Seth concentrated, reaching out with his mind toward Emily. He could still feel her, fighting beneath Sebastian's influence. If he could just break through again, stronger this time...

Sebastian's hand shot out, gripping Seth's throat with impossible strength. "Your newfound abilities are impressive, but crude. Untrained." The vampire's fingers tightened. "You think a few days of enhancement can match *centuries* of power?"

Black spots danced in Seth's vision as his airway constricted. He clawed at Sebastian's hand, but it might as well have been carved from marble. The vampire lifted him effortlessly, feet dangling above the floor.

"I could kill you now," Sebastian said conversationally. "But that would waste the potential you represent. No, you'll complete the biography as planned. Your resistance makes you more valuable, not less."

"I know you won't kill me." Seth managed to say between ragged gasps for air, "It would take too long for you to recruit another biographer. You said I'm the seventh and that's significant to you somehow."

A new sensation bloomed in Seth's mind as oxygen deprivation set in, not pain, but clarity. Sebastian's physical contact had opened a channel between them. Through it, Seth caught flashes of the vampire's thoughts. He saw a circular chamber lined with manuscripts, Emily strapped to an altar, blood flowing into ancient channels, power building toward some cataclysmic transformation.

The vision ended as suddenly as it began when Sebastian released him. Seth collapsed to the floor, gasping for air.

"Fascinating," Sebastian murmured, studying Seth with renewed interest. "You saw it, didn't you? A glimpse of what awaits."

Seth coughed, massaging his bruised throat. "You're planning some kind of ritual."

"Not planning. Completing." Sebastian straightened his suit jacket with fastidious care. "The final phase of a process begun years ago, when I chose my first biographer. Each writer contributed their essence to the work, their passion, their creative force, their life energy."

"You killed them," Seth rasped. "All of them."

"Their deaths were necessary transformations. As yours will be." Sebastian moved toward the door. "Complete the biography, Seth. Make it your finest work. When it's done, you'll understand your true purpose."

"I won't help you," Seth said, struggling to his feet.

"You already have." Sebastian gestured to Seth's laptop, still open on the desk. "Every word you've written has been a step toward the Ascension. Even your resistance feeds the process in its own way."

Emily appeared in the doorway again, her face expressionless. "The car is waiting, Sebastian."

Sebastian nodded. "Excellent, my dear." He turned back to Seth. "Don't do anything foolish while we're gone. Your part in this isn't finished yet."

As they turned to leave, Seth gathered his strength and focused it into one desperate mental push. "Emily!" he called, both aloud and with his mind. "Fight him!"

Emily paused, half-turning. For a second, the real Emily surfaced again, frightened, confused, but fighting. "Help me," she whispered, her eyes clear and present.

Sebastian snarled, wrapping an arm around her waist and pulling her away. The door slammed shut with supernatural force, the wood splintering around the jamb.

Seth staggered to the door, yanking it open with some effort. The hallway was empty, as if they'd vanished into thin air. He reached out with his new senses, trying to track the dark energy of Sebastian's aura, but it was already fading, moving beyond his range. He slammed his fist flat into the splintered door, "Damn, not strong enough yet."

His phone buzzed. It was a text from Connie: "What happened? Our instruments detected a massive energy spike near your location."

Seth typed back with shaking fingers: "Sebastian took Emily. They're leaving for Vienna tonight. He's planning something called the Chronicler's Ascension."

The response came instantly: "Get to the Society NOW. It's worse than we thought."

Seth grabbed his jacket and Winston's journal from its hiding place. As he turned to leave, his gaze fell on his laptop screen. The biography document was open, though he didn't remember leaving it that way. New text scrolled across the page, typing itself as he watched:

"The seventh biographer will complete the circle. His resistance will make the Ascension all the sweeter. The sacrifice has begun."

The words vanished as suddenly as they had appeared, leaving no trace in the document. But Seth knew what he'd seen. Sebastian was already using him, connecting to him through the biography itself. The manuscript wasn't just a book, it was a conduit, a magical link between writer and subject. Sabastian had been using mysticism and technology to invent this new ritual he planned.

Fifteen minutes later, Seth burst into the Society headquarters, still gasping for breath from his run across the city. Higgins and Connie met him in the entrance hall, their faces grim.

"Tell us everything," Higgins said, leading Seth toward the library.

Seth recounted the confrontation, his partial success in reaching Emily, Sebastian's revelation about the Chronicler's Ascension, and his plans to take Emily to Vienna.

"I was afraid of this," Higgins said when Seth finished. "The signs have been there for decades, but we never connected them to Sebastian specifically."

"Connected what?" Seth demanded. "What is this Ascension he's planning?"

Higgins exchanged a look with Connie. "It's an ancient ritual, predating modern vampirism. A way for certain bloodlines to ascend to a higher state of power. The original ritual was deemed impossible to recreate in the modern age. There is no one left who knows how the ritual's magic worked, but if what you said was true, he has found a way to revive it using technology in place of the ancient forgotten magic required."

"And it also requires seven biographers," Seth said. "I'm the seventh."

"Not just biographers," Connie clarified. "Chroniclers, writers who tell the vampire's true story. The ritual harnesses the creative energy, the passion that goes into capturing a life in words. It's the reason he's been so particular about your words."

"The compulsion to tell stories is one of humanity's oldest impulses," Higgins added. "There's power in that storytelling, power vampires of Sebastian's lineage have learned to harvest and redirect. It is a kin to writing the name of a demon or angel to give yourself power over them. Letters on paper are just symbols you have trained your brain to interpret and understand. Those symbols are ancient and have power."

"Words are comprised of symbols?" Seth said, "you mean like pentagrams, or any other symbol used in ritual."

"Yes." Higgins said. "Sabastian is more than a bloodsucker, much more."

"If he is this type of vampire, he will also need a journal written by his own hand." Connie said. "Something he wrote as a false narrative about himself and his kind. It will make him look less like a predator and more like a victim of dire circumstances."

"Why?" Seth asked.

"Because his journal is the counterbalance intended to be used against you. It will never see publication, but it should still exist. If you could find it and destroy it, then it would increase your power over him, and his over you with diminish."

"I will keep my eyes open."

Connie opened an old book on the table, "Ah, here it is. He doesn't need to carry it with him. He can have it put up in a safe place. That means you might be able to find it."

"Yes, he most likely would not risk carrying it with him on a trip to Europe. That would allow too many variables. It could be lost in luggage or destroyed in some other way. He would keep it locked away somewhere safe." Higgins added.

Seth thought of the vision he'd glimpsed in Sebastian's mind, the circular chamber, the altar, Emily's body. "He's taking Emily to use in the ritual somehow."

"I'm afraid not just to use," Higgins said gravely. "To transform. The Ascension requires a witness who is neither fully human nor fully vampire, someone in the transition state."

"He's turning her," Seth whispered. "Why in the transition state?"

"Partially," Connie confirmed. "The ritual requires someone caught between worlds, because they are able to perceive both realities, and they are not yet strong enough to challenge his power."

"And once the ritual is complete?" Seth asked, though he already suspected the answer.

"If successful, Sebastian will achieve a state no vampire has reached in millennia," Higgins said. "Immunity to traditional vampire weaknesses like sunlight, religious symbols, holy water, invitation thresholds, all of it. The ability to glamour not just individuals but masses. He would become something beyond a vampire; he would be a demigod."

"I have never seen a movie or read a book with a vampire like that! One who feeds on blood, the suffering of others, and creativity."

"No, and you never will." Connie said, "You can't produce a work including someone like Sabastian. That's how they have stayed in the shadows for so long. People have tried and found out the hard way how the creativity and enjoyment of the people reading it or watching it gave the vampire power. Especially in written form as the symbolism of the letters are far more powerful."

"One such film was produced in the 19 teens, but it was destroyed by fire once it was discovered it was feeding the vampire it depicted." Higgins said.

This wasn't just about saving Emily anymore or exposing Sebastian's crimes. This was about preventing something that could alter the balance between human and supernatural worlds forever.

"If the society knows so much about monsters like Sabastian, then it must also know how we can stop him." Seth said.

"It's a bit unclear because this hasn't happened in so long, but I know one thing we must do. We must go to Vienna," Connie said firmly. "Tonight."

"Not just Vienna," Higgins corrected. "We follow them wherever the ritual leads. We prevent the Ascension at all costs."

"And Emily?" Seth looked between them. "Can she be saved if he's already begun turning her?"

Higgins hesitated. "There are accounts of interrupted transformations. Some failed, leaving the subject neither human nor vampire. It left them in a tortured half-existence. Others reverted to human form, though they were never quite the same."

"But it's possible," Seth pressed. "She can be saved."

"It's possible," Higgins conceded. "But you must be prepared for the possibility that the Emily you knew is already gone."

Seth shook his head. "I refuse. I reached her today. She's still fighting. I'm not giving up on her."

"Then we have preparations to make," Connie said, her voice taking on a military precision. "Weapons, artifacts, protective gear. The Society has resources in Europe, but we'll need to move quickly."

"We'll need to pull some field agents from their missions to help us." Higgins said.

"I can still feel her," Seth said, interrupting Higgins and Connie's planning. "The link I created. I know it's still there."

Higgins looked surprised. "That shouldn't be possible across such distance, not for someone with your limited experience."

"It's there," Seth insisted. "And if I can feel her..."

"It has to be residual energy." Higgins said. "I only *just* performed the ritual to release your abilities."

"Didn't you say during the ritual that you can do anything you want but it's your brain that tells you that you can't?"

"Yes." Higgins said.

"Well, it's not telling me I can't do this anymore."

"Then you might be able to help her resist Sebastian's influence from within," Connie finished, excitement in her voice. "Even as they travel."

"Or track them if they change destination," Higgins added thoughtfully. "We can find them though you like a GPS tracker!"

Seth closed his eyes again, concentrating on the faint connection. For just a moment, he felt Emily's consciousness brush against his. She was terrified but defiant, holding onto her humanity with desperate strength.

"Hold on," he whispered, willing his reassurance through the link. "We're coming for you."

Somewhere over the Atlantic, Emily Laurence sat rigid in a private jet's leather seat, her face a mask of forced calm. Beside her, Sebastian Wolfram smiled at what he sensed, a feeble connection reaching across miles, a futile attempt at rescue.

"The biographer is persistent," he remarked, sipping from a crystal glass filled with dark red liquid. "But it changes nothing. Even if he plans to follow us, by the time he reaches Vienna, you'll be ready for your role in the Ascension."

Inside her mind, where Sebastian's control couldn't quite reach, Emily clung to the faint warmth of Seth's presence like a drowning woman to a lifeline. She had no way to respond, no way to send a message back through.

But she could listen. And wait. And prepare for the moment when Sebastian's guard might drop, even for an instant.

Chapter 14
Making Plans, Making Moves

Seth stood in the center of Sebastian's penthouse, the silence was unbearable, but he knew true silence was a ruse. There was no such thing as silence, only the lack of the ability to hear everything. The vampire's scent lingered, that peculiar blend of aged leather, spice, and something metallic that Seth now recognized as most likely being blood. With Sebastian and Emily gone to Europe, the apartment felt like an abandoned stage set, waiting for its actors to return.

He moved methodically through the rooms, searching for anything that might help him understand what Sebastian had planned. The ritual, this Chronicler's Ascension, required seven biographers. He knew he was the seventh. He was the final piece the fiend needed. What he didn't know was if he had to be living or dead. He knew the others were already dead, but then again, he didn't know if they were dead, turned into vampires, or what. He hoped he wouldn't have to be turned. Being a vampire seemed like a miserable existence and even if what Wolf, that is Sabastian, planned worked it still seemed like it would be miserable.

In the study, Seth ran his fingers along the bookshelves, pausing at titles that seemed significant and pulling on them or pushing them in. Hidden compartments where always behind the bookshelves in the movies. He had a thought, maybe he could use his newly enhanced sense. He concentrated on what he reasoned might work and put his hand on the books and along the walls. His finger tingled as he approached a particular section of the wall. Something felt... off. Not quite visible to normal perception, but there, nonetheless. It shimmered before his eyes, a subtle wrongness in the air hovering over a spot near the wall.

"What are you hiding?" Seth murmured, pressing his palms against the wood paneling.

He closed his eyes, focusing on the sensation. Since the ritual at the Society, his awareness had expanded in ways he was still discovering. Now, he concentrated on that strange feeling, letting it guide his perception deeper. He could see inside the wall with his mind's eye.

Seth let his finger trace the pattern of the wood grain until they found a nearly invisible seam. He pressed, and a small section of paneling slid aside, revealing a narrow crevice within the wall. He held up his hands in front of his face, "This is really cool!"

The smell hit him first, copper and salt, the unmistakable scent of blood, old blood. Many victims' blood layered over years. Seth recoiled instinctively, then forced himself to look closer.

Inside the crevice lay a book, bound in what appeared to be ancient leather or at least a thick aged, pulpy paper he had not encountered ever before. The cover was in an older style like it might have been from the nineteenth century.

He reached for it, then hesitated. The air around the book shimmered with a protective barrier. Sebastian had sealed his secret with the blood of his victims, creating a ward that would normally render the book undetectable.

"But I can see you, can't I" Seth whispered, focusing his will against the barrier.

The resistance felt like pushing through thick mud, but Seth persisted, channeling his will. His fingers brushed leather, and a jolt of cold energy shot up his arm. Images flashed through his mind. He saw faces contorted in terror, bodies drained of life, Sebastian standing over them with bloody hands and a satisfied smile.

Seth gritted his teeth and grabbed the book, pulling it free from its hiding place. The barrier shattered with an audible snapping noise.

The title appeared on the cover as if written in fresh ink: "Shrouded in Shadows."

"Got you," Seth breathed, tucking the journal into his bag.

Two hours later, Seth placed the journal on the polished oak table in the Society's library. Higgins, Connie, and two other

Society members he hadn't met before gathered around, their faces grave.

"This is it," Seth said. "Sebastian's personal journal. It was hidden in his apartment, protected by blood magic."

"You shouldn't have been able to sense it," one of the strangers remarked, an elderly woman with sharp eyes and silver hair. "The blood of victims creates a powerful concealment."

"My abilities have been... evolving," Seth admitted. "Ever since the ritual."

Higgins nodded thoughtfully. "The unlocking process affects each person differently. Your natural resistance to Sebastian may have created a particular sensitivity to his magic."

"It's almost too much to believe." The older man said. "No one has taken to the ritual like that in decades. I looked. The last one who developed abilities against the unknown this fast was Thaddeus Rose himself."

"The founder?" Seth asked.

"One of them." The old man replied.

Higgins cupped his chin, "If I'm not mistaken, Nigel, that happened to Rose when the entities were trying infiltrate his private school, Wytchmore. That was also a harrowing time. Perhaps providence is lending us a hand in such strained times."

Nigel agreed with a nod. "It wasn't Rose himself though, it was one of his grandchildren I believe, or it might have been one of the Ravenscroft family. I can't remember. The shadow attacks happened to one of them at Wytchmore a few years after Thaddeus Rose died."

Connie reached for the journal, touched it, then pulled back with a hiss. "It's cold. Like touching ice."

"Of course. You know it's more than a book," Higgins explained, donning a pair of thin gloves before carefully opening the cover.

"It is? Nigel asked. "How so?"

"It's a focus for Sebastian's power. It's a counterbalance to the biographies he commissions."

Nigel leaned forward. "I have lived all these years, and I have never seen something such as this. What is its meaning?"

"The Chronicler's Ascension requires balance," the silver-haired woman explained. "The biographer writes the public story, capturing the vampire's essence through an outside perspective. But the vampire must also chronicle their own journey. It's the shadow narrative that rarely if ever sees publication. It's usually a watered-down account designed to make the vampire look good. A victim of evil doers who wish to destroy his kind."

"Together, they create a magical circuit," Higgins continued, turning pages filled with elegant, archaic handwriting. "The public biography channels creative energy from readers to the vampire. The private journal focuses and directs that energy toward the Ascension and to the vampires living life force."

"So destroying it would stop the ritual?" Seth asked.

"Not quite," Connie said. "The journal must be destroyed by fire in Sebastian's presence. Otherwise, he can simply create another to take its place."

"The destruction must occur at a specific moment in the ritual," Higgins added. "When Sebastian attempts to complete the circuit between his journal and your biography."

"So we need to fly to Vienna, find Sebastian, interrupt his ritual, and destroy his journal at exactly the right moment." Seth concluded.

"While also rescuing Emily," Connie reminded him.

"And preventing Sebastian from killing us all," the silver-haired woman added dryly.

"This kind of vampire is a might complicated." Nigel said.

Seth nodded, determination hardening within him. "We'd better start planning the trip."

While the others wondered off to the computer station to begin the travel plans, Seth stayed at the table and stared at Sebastian's journal. The leather-bound book seemed to call out to him. He resisted. Then, almost unconsciously, he reached out and touched the cover again.

The room disappeared.

Blood and fire filled his vision. A circular chamber with seven alcoves, each containing a writing desk. Six of the alcoves contained ghostly figures bent over manuscripts, their essence slowly draining into the center of the place where a crystalline structure illumined the room with crimson light. The seventh alcove remained empty, waiting.

"Seth!" Connie's voice pulled him back. "Your nose is bleeding."

Seth touched his face, fingers coming away red. "I saw it. The ritual chamber. Six writers... already there somehow. Spirits or echoes, trapped."

Higgins leaned forward, alarmed. "The journal is attempting to make connect with you. As the seventh biographer, you're the final component."

"There's more," Seth said, his voice hollow. "Sebastian isn't just trying to become more powerful. He's trying to resurrect something. Something ancient and terrible." he shook his head and scoffed, "This is the darndest thing I have ever seen in my life. A vampire like this is not supposed to exist. According to lore they stalk their prey in the night and suck their blood for sustenance. They don't do strange rituals, and they don't feed on emotion and literature!"

Higgins put his hand on Seth's shoulder. "There are many versions of vampire. We just call them vampires as a catch-all. Many vampires leech emotions and psychic energy and they don't even need blood at all. Others, leech minerals, especially salt, from their victims. For other vampires, it's iron from their victim's blood."

"Salt? That's everywhere. They can get it from a saltshaker." Seth said.

"Ah, but they must get it from human blood. It doesn't work any other way. We don't know why but we have scientists working on it. The only vampires who do not suck blood is the psychic variety. This bastard you have been in tangled with has learned how to get what he needs from many sources. He wants to circumvent the drawbacks of being a vampire."

"That's right." Connie said. "These old vampires realize the price of immortality and start looking for things like rituals, different sources of sustenance, and so forth just like a human scientist might look for a cure to a disease. They seek to change their circumstances after so many years, so they may live their lives on their own terms instead of under the limitations of their kind."

The older man, Nigel, cleared his throat. "I am more interested in that ancient evil he brought up rather than a lesson on vampire kin. We can fill him in on the particulars of vampire lore later. What do you think he is conjuring, young man?"

"I don't know. It just seemed...ancient and evil."

The silver-haired woman paled. "The Elder."

"What elder?" Connie asked.

"Not what, who," Nigel replied. "If she's right, Sebastian is attempting to resurrect the progenitor of his bloodline, Mortus the Ravager. A being old when Rome was young."

Seth's phone buzzed with a message that made him instantly nervous:

"I know you took it. You've activated the binding. Now your fate is sealed. The journal will find its way back to me, and you with it. -S"

The lights in the Society headquarters flickered ominously.

"We need to move. Now," Seth said. "Sebastian may have planted a way to sense the journal."

As if in response, the book suddenly burst into flames that didn't consume it.

"Containment protocol!" Higgins shouted. Two Society members rushed forward with a lead-lined box, slamming it over the journal. The flames died instantly.

"Vienna is a trap," Seth realized. "It's misdirection. He's not going there at all."

"Then where?" Connie asked.

Seth closed his eyes, reaching through his connection to Emily. Past Sebastian's interference, he caught a single fleeting image from her mind: a castle perched on the edge of a cliff, waves crashing below.

"Coastal. Old. A castle…"

"His home, his Lair," the silver-haired woman whispered. "Sebastian's original turning ground in Cornwall."

"That's our true destination," Higgins declared. "And we have less time than we thought."

Seth rose from his chair. "Then we need to be ready. Sebastian thinks he's manipulating me, using me as the final piece in his ritual. But he's made one crucial mistake."

"What's that?" Connie asked.

"He taught me how the stories he needs work." Seth said. "How narratives can be shaped, molded to serve a purpose. Now I'm going to write an ending he never saw coming."

"I still want to know why he wants to raise the elder." The silver haired woman said.

Higgins sniffed, "You all finish the preparations for the trip. I will research this elder and see why that bastard vampire wants to bring him here to this realm."

Chapter 15
of Words and Blood

Seth stared out the small oval window of the chartered flight, watching the clouds drift beneath them. The Society had spared no expense, chartering a private jet, arranging for diplomatic clearance, bringing along equipment that would have raised eyebrows at any commercial security checkpoint. The North Atlantic stretched endlessly below, a dark expanse separating them from their destination.

"How's the connection holding?" Connie asked, sliding into the seat across from him.

Seth closed his eyes, focusing on the tenuous link to Emily. "Still there. Weaker than before, but I can feel her fighting."

He'd been maintaining contact in short bursts, afraid that prolonged connection might alert Sebastian to their change in plans. Each time he reached out, Emily's consciousness felt more distant, more fragmented, but still unmistakably her.

"You should rest," Connie suggested, nodding toward the leather-bound journal secured in a lead-lined case between them. "We've got hours before landing."

Seth eyed Sebastian's journal warily. Since its dramatic flare-up at the Society headquarters, the book had remained dormant, but he could feel its presence like a cold spot in the cabin, a void pulling at his awareness.

"I need to understand what we're facing," he said, reaching for the case.

Connie's hand shot out, gripping his wrist. "Be careful. That thing is connected to him."

"I know." Seth met her gaze steadily. "But it's also our best weapon."

With gloved hands, he carefully extracted the journal from its protective casing. The leather felt unnaturally cold even through the barrier of the gloves. Opening to the first page, Seth began to read.

April 17, 1794 – I write these words with hands that no longer feel like my own. Three nights have passed since my rebirth, since Lady Eleanor found me walking home from Thornfield Farm and offered me shelter from the storm. I was but a farmer's hand, covered in mud and reeking of livestock. Why she chose me, I cannot fathom...

Seth looked up, smirking. "He lied about when he was turned. This says 1794, not World War II."

Higgins leaned over from the adjacent seat. "Not surprising. Vampires often create false histories to obscure their true origins. Even this story is probably fabricated."

Seth quickly filled him in, "he's been careless with his stories. Not long after he told me he was turned during World War II, he began telling me of events he supposedly experienced much earlier, thousands of years actually."

"What did he hope to accomplish by such a blatant error. The readers would catch that immediately." Higgins said.

"It was a test for me. He wanted to see how I would handle the writing. He wanted to find out if I would write exactly what he told me to write or question him or make changes without his authorization." Seth explained. "Of course, he never intended for the biography to ever see the light of day."

Seth continued reading, skimming through decades of Sebastian's private thoughts. The journal painted a picture vastly different from the sophisticated, controlled predator Seth had come to know. The early entries revealed a frightened young man of twenty, born in 1774 to poverty, transformed against his will, and abandoned by his maker to navigate immortality alone.

June 3, 1801 – Seven years of this cursed existence. I did not ask for this life. I did not seek immortality or power. It was thrust upon me by a creature who saw me as nothing more than amusement, then discarded me when I failed to provide adequate entertainment.

Page after page documented Sebastian's struggle with his nature, his resentment toward humanity, his growing belief that his victimhood justified any action necessary to improve his condition.

November 12, 1923 – I have found a way. The texts speak of an Ascension, a means by which our kind may transcend the limitations imposed upon us. The hunger that never ceases, the weaknesses that plague us, the isolation that stretches through centuries, all might be overcome. If this existence was forced upon me, am I not entitled to better it by any means necessary?

A sudden jolt of pain shot through Seth's temple. He gasped, dropping the journal onto the table.

"Seth?" Connie's voice sounded distant through the ringing in his ears.

A flood of images cascaded through his mind; it was a vision of Emily in a stone chamber, Sebastian arranging manuscripts on pedestals, and blood dripping into channels carved in the floor.

"He has them," Seth gasped. "The manuscripts. All of them."

"What manuscripts?" Higgins asked sharply.

"From the other biographers. The unfinished ones." Seth pressed his palms against his temples, trying to sort through the jumble of images Emily had somehow pushed through their connection. "He's been collecting them. Each one contains... part of them, their essence, their souls trapped inside their work."

"The components for the ritual," Higgins murmured. "We suspected as much."

"There's more," Seth continued, the pain intensifying as he forced himself to hold the connection. "He has the final pages for each manuscript. He's going to complete them all during the ritual."

The connection snapped suddenly, leaving Seth disoriented and nauseous. Blood trickled from his nose, spattering onto his shirt.

"That's enough," the silver-haired woman named Beth, Seth had recently learned, said firmly. "Your abilities are developing too rapidly. It's dangerous."

"I'm fine," Seth insisted, wiping the blood away with the back of his hand. "That was emily sending me an image."

"No, it most certainly was not." Beth said. I have studied the abilities of the unknown my entire life. One who has not been awakened by the ritual, as you have been, cannot send any kind of message back though the connection. Their brains still tell them they can't do a thing and so they can't. It requires someone like Higgins to open the mind."

"She's right and You're not fine," Higgins said, his expression grave. "It was you picking up on residual energy from what Emily must have seen. You must be careful. No one develops abilities at this rate without consequences. Not since Thaddeus Rose himself."

"Thaddeus Rose?" Seth repeated. "The founder again, right?"

"One of them." Nigel answered grinning. You really must commit that knowledge to memory."

"Yeah, I seem to have a problem with that. What happened to Mr. Rose?"

"He developed extraordinary abilities in a matter of weeks. By the end, he could perceive things no human was meant to see." Nigel said.

"And it drove him mad," Beth finished. "His final years were spent in isolation, his mind fractured by what he'd witnessed."

The cabin fell silent. Seth was touched by their concern. It had been a while since anyone had even acted like they cared about his wellbeing.

"We need to discuss whether this is safe," Nigel said finally, addressing Higgins rather than Seth. "If his connections to Sebastian and the girl are both growing stronger, if his abilities are developing unchecked..."

"I'm right here," Seth snapped. "And I'm not going to go mad before we save Emily. My connection is to her, by the way. I don't have a connection to Sabastian."

"Don't be so certain." Higgins warned.

"Plus, you can say you will not go mad all you want but it doesn't make it so. It's not exactly your decision is it," Beth replied firmly. "I feel it's my duty to inform you the Society has protocols for situations like this."

"Situations like what?" Seth demanded. "Like me?"

"Like any asset who becomes a potential liability," Higgins said carefully.

"Your connection to Emily is also your connection to Sabastian." Nigel muttered. Seth knew the older man felt strongly about getting the correction in while it was still relevant in the conversation.

Seth leaned back in his seat, acknowledging Connie's concerned expression. "You're right. I should rest." He closed his eyes, feigning relaxation while thinking about his rapidly evolving mental abilities. The Society members' worried glances hadn't escaped his notice. They saw him as a liability now, a potential danger to their mission.

Once their attention shifted to their own interests, Seth allowed his breathing to slow, creating the impression of sleep. But instead of resting, he turned his focus inward, searching for that tenuous connection to Emily he'd felt earlier.

He had no idea what he was doing. The ritual had unlocked abilities he still barely understood, let alone control. He let his instinct guide him now, a sense that the connection between him and Emily existed beyond physical distance or Sebastian's interference.

Seth visualized the link as a silver thread stretching across the Atlantic, fragile but unbroken. He concentrated on following it, pushing his consciousness along its length. The cabin around him faded from his awareness as he traveled the connection, seeking out Emily.

At first, there was nothing but darkness and the distant roar of the aircraft engines. Then, like tuning into a radio station through static, he felt her presence.

Emily? He projected the thought, uncertain if she could hear him.

The response wasn't words but a wave of emotion so powerful it made his physical body jerk in his seat. Terror. Pain. Desperation. Her pain tugged at his heart. He knew she probably still loved him; Sabastian had asserted his will upon her. It wasn't her fault she was compelled to be with Sabastian over him. At least that's what he wanted to believe.

He concentrated. The darkness in his mind's eye gave way to fragmented images. There were stone walls, flickering torchlight, and Sebastian's face looming close. Too close.

Seth pushed harder, strengthening the connection. The images sharpened, coalescing into a horrifying scene: Emily pinned against a wall, her head tilted back, eyes wide with fear and something else. There was a sense of a terrible, unwilling ecstasy. Sebastian's mouth was at her throat, his hands gripping her arms with inhuman strength.

Seth! is that you? Are you there? Help me! Her mental voice crashed into his consciousness, raw with panic. *He's feeding on me! I can feel myself slipping away!*

How was this possible? Beth had just told him Emily could not answer his mental messages. It must be Sabastian! He is connected to her both mentally and physically. Her transformation through him must have allowed it.

He had a thought from his childhood. He and some friends had read a book about the CIA and remote viewing. They used to lie in bed at night and try to astral project to each other's rooms. It never worked but it was fun trying. He thought maybe now it would be possible with his new abilities. He tried it. He left her mind and body and saw the room from above. He floated down next to the couple.

Seth watched in horror as Sebastian's teeth sank deeper into Emily's neck, blood trickling down her pale skin. The vampire's eyes were closed in rapture, his expression one of obscene pleasure as he drank.

I'm coming, Seth promised, pouring all his determination into the thought. *Hold on, Emily. Fight him!*

Sebastian's head suddenly snapped up, blood staining his lips. His eyes wide open, scanning the empty air as if sensing an intruder.

"Who's there?" the vampire hissed, his voice audible across the connection, his un-retracted teeth making him lisp.

Seth could suddenly sense Emily in a panic. *He can sense you...go!*

Sebastian's gaze locked onto Emily's face, comprehension dawning. "The biographer," he snarled. "Still interfering."

He grabbed Emily's chin, forcing her to look at him. "Tell your would-be rescuer what happens when someone tries to take what's mine."

Sebastian's hand moved to Emily's throat, squeezing. Seth felt her panic spike, felt her struggling to breathe.

No! Seth mentally shouted, rage and fear propelling him deeper into the connection. Without knowing how, he pushed back against Sebastian's presence, trying to force the vampire away from Emily.

For a moment, it seemed to work. Sebastian staggered back a step, his expression shocked. But then his face contorted with fury.

"You think your newfound abilities can challenge me?" Sebastian snarled, looking directly at Seth though the connection. "Watch what happens when you meddle in affairs beyond your understanding."

He yanked Emily forward and bit down on her neck again, harder this time. Seth felt her pain as if it were his own, felt her consciousness dimming as Sebastian drank deeply.

"No!" Seth screamed, the word tearing from his physical throat as his body convulsed in the airplane seat.

The connection shattered. Seth's eyes flew open to find the Society members gathered around him, faces lined with alarm. Blood poured from his nose and ears, soaking his shirt collar.

"He's feeding on her!" Seth gasped, struggling to rise despite the hands holding him down. "That monster is draining her!"

"Seth, calm down," Higgins ordered, pressing him back into the seat. "You're hemorrhaging."

"We need to sedate him," Beth said, already preparing a syringe she had just pulled from her oversized purse.

"No!" Seth fought against their restraining hands. "You don't understand. He knows we're coming. He's hurting her to punish me for interfering."

"Your nose is bleeding profusely," Connie said, pressing a cloth to his face. "And your ears—this is exactly what we warned you about."

"I don't care!" Seth's voice went hoarse with desperation. "Emily is dying right now while we're stuck on this plane!"

Nigel exchanged a grim look with Higgins. "The connection is too dangerous. It's destroying him from the inside out."

"And it's giving away our position," Beth added. "If Sebastian sensed him, he knows we're coming." She plunged the needle into his arm without so much as a twitch or a swab of alcohol. The cold liquid flowed into his arm and into his blood stream. A moment later and everything went hazy.

Chapter 16
The Fortress by the Sea

Seth's head pounded as the Society's Range Rover bounced along the narrow coastal road. The sedative had worn off a couple of hours ago, leaving him with a throbbing headache and a bitter taste in his mouth. He had no idea how they managed to get him into the car from the plane. Through the window, he watched gray waves crash against jagged cliffs; the landscape was as bleak as his mood.

"There it is," Higgins said, pointing to a dark silhouette perched on a distant promontory. "Wolfram Castle."

Seth leaned forward, squinting against the fading daylight. The castle rose from the cliff like it had been carved from the rock itself with its sharp angles and weathered stone, a single tower reaching toward the leaden sky. Even from this distance, it radiated a sense of ancient malevolence. "It looks like something you would see in an old horror film."

"It probably *has* been in a couple." Beth said.

"Emily's in there," Seth murmured, instinctively reaching for their connection.

Nothing. Where once he'd felt her presence, frightened but fighting, was now replaced with emptiness. Sebastian had somehow severed their link, isolating Emily's consciousness from his reach.

"Don't," Connie warned, noticing his expression. "I know you're worried about her after what you saw, but remember, you nearly died on the plane."

Seth nodded reluctantly. The memory of Sebastian's fury when he'd detected Seth's presence was still fresh in his memory. The vampire would be expecting another attempt, and he would be prepared to counter it. Only this time, perhaps he would make his anger fatal.

The Range Rover turned off the main road, following a rutted track to a small fishing village nestled in a protected cove below the castle. Whitewashed cottages huddled together against the wind, smoke curling from stone chimneys. It looked like time had forgotten this place.

"Our contact has secured lodgings," Higgins explained as they pulled up to a weathered building with a faded sign reading "The Mariner's Rest." "We'll establish our base here."

Inside, the pub's common room was warm and dim, smelling of wood smoke and ale. A handful of locals glanced up as they entered, then quickly returned to their drinks. Seth sensed their wariness and knew instantly strangers weren't welcome here, especially not strangers asking questions about the castle on the cliff.

"I'll check the surveillance equipment," Beth said, heading upstairs with several heavy cases.

"I'll speak with our local informant," Higgins added. "Connie, get Seth settled."

Seth followed Connie to a corner table, his legs still unsteady from the sedative. Through the window, he could see the castle silhouetted against the darkening sky. Emily was up there, alone with that monster, possibly being drained of her humanity with each passing hour. He tried not to think about it too much, but the image of that bastard feeding on her stuck in his mind.

"We'll get her back," Connie said, reading his expression.

"How?" Seth's voice went hoarse again. "Sebastian knows we're coming. He's cut my connection to Emily. The castle is probably crawling with his allies and minions."

"Beth's initial scan showed at least a dozen heat signatures," Connie confirmed. "Human servants, most likely. And there are colder spots moving among them, which are likely lesser vampires."

Seth buried his face in his hands. "I can't feel her anymore, Connie. It's like she's just... gone."

"Sebastian's performing isolation spells," came a voice from behind them. "Cutting her off from any external influence."

"Spells?" Seth asked. "Like a wizard or something?"

"No, like the dark glamouring magic of a vampire."

Seth whirled around. He knew that voice! A thin man in shabby clothes stood there, his face half-hidden by a worn cap. It took Seth a moment to recognize him.

"Nathan Pike," he breathed. "From the coffee shop in New York."

Nathan glanced nervously around the pub before sliding into the seat beside them. "I've been tracking Sebastian for months. When I heard rumors about the Chronicler's Ascension, I knew he'd return here. I also knew someone would be following him."

"You worked for him," Seth said. "For decades."

Nathan nodded, his eyes haunted. "Fifty years I served that monster. Watched what he did to people like you. I saw what he did to writers, artists, and other creative souls."

"Why is he doing this?" Seth asked. "What does he gain from the Ascension?" He already knew the answer but he asked anyway in hopes Pike would give him more insight, or tip his hand if he wasn't on the up and up.

"Power," Nathan replied simply. "Freedom from the limitations of his kind. But more than that he seeks validation. He believes his suffering entitles him to transcendence. But I know with whom you travel. I suspect you already know all that."

"His suffering?" Seth scoffed. "He's the one causing all the pain."

"That's his key vulnerability," Nathan leaned closer, lowering his voice. "Sebastian feeds on misery and despair. The negative emotions of creative minds sustain him, they fuel his power. That's why he chooses biographers who are struggling financially, emotionally, and spiritually. He cultivates their suffering, and then he harvests it."

Seth thought of his own situation when Sebastian had approached him. He was broke, his career was stalled, and he was desperate for a breakthrough. The perfect target.

"And Emily?" he asked. "I suppose she's merely a tool to add to my anguish?"

"Yes, correct. She's a tool for certain," Nathan said bluntly. "A way to deepen your suffering. He took her to ensure you'd never find happiness during the writing process. No matter how much you tried to move past it, seeing her with him would always bring you back to misery and anger."

"So what's his weakness?" Connie asked.

"The opposite emotions, like happiness, and wellbeing," Nathan replied. "Joy. Success. Genuine contentment. These emotions are toxic to him. They disrupt his ability to feed. But I will warn you. It's not enough to pretend or force positive thoughts. You can't merely think happy thoughts or go to your happy place." There was a copious amount of sarcasm in his voice. "You must truly feel them and even more so you must believe you feel them."

Seth laughed bitterly. "That's why he took Emily from me. Even if I tried to be happy, how could I when I know she's suffering because of me?"

"Exactly," Nathan nodded. "He's calculated everything perfectly. Your misery feeds him, strengthens him. And with each biographer he's consumed, his ability to manipulate emotions has grown stronger."

"Why couldn't he just be a normal vampire? No, he has to have extra psychic feeding habits." Seth lamented. He stared out at the darkening castle. Sebastian had orchestrated everything from the beginning like choosing him for his vulnerabilities, taking Emily to deepen his despair, isolating her consciousness to prevent any rescue attempt.

"The bastard knows exactly what he's doing," Seth muttered, a cold determination settling in his chest. "But so do I."

Seth paced the length of the small cottage the Society had rented as their base of operations. Rain beat down hard against the windows. The howling wind making him believe more and more he was stuck in a nineteen thirties horror film. The weather matched his mood, which was dark, turbulent, and unpredictable.

The door burst open. Two Society members half-carried, half-dragged a third between them. Blood soaked through the man's jacket, his face ashen. Nathan Pike was with them. He closed the door against the weather as they entered.

"Janssen!" Higgins rushed forward, clearing maps from the table. "Put him here. What happened?"

They laid the wounded scout on the table. Seth recognized him. He was a quiet, efficient man who'd volunteered to monitor the castle's perimeter.

"Vampire sentries," Janssen gasped, wincing as Beth cut away his jacket to reveal three deep gashes across his chest. "They're… everywhere now. It wasn't like this yesterday."

Seth moved closer. "Did you see Emily?"

Janssen nodded weakly. "North tower. Glimpsed her through a window. She looked different."

"Different how?" Seth demanded, earning a sharp look from Beth as she worked to clean the wounds.

"Pale. She was far too pale if you asked me." Janssen coughed, blood speckling his lips.

"He's turning her." Higgins said. He looked at Seth nervously and then lowered his head, "Sorry, I forget myself."

Seth said nothing.

"What else?" Connie asked.

"Sebastian! He was preparing something in the great hall. Artifacts, manuscripts arranged in a circle."

Higgins and Connie exchanged alarmed glances.

"The ritual," Connie whispered. "He's accelerating the timeline."

"How soon?" Seth asked.

"Three days," Janssen managed before Beth administered a sedative. "The lunar eclipse. I heard the servants talking about it. It hasn't happened here in quite a while."

Seth turned to the window, staring out at the distant silhouette of Sebastian's castle perched on the cliff edge. Three days. Just seventy-two hours to prepare, to save Emily before Sebastian completed his transformation and achieved the Ascension.

"We need a new approach," Higgins said, spreading a weathered map across a side table. "Direct assault is suicide with his forces increased."

"What about these?" Connie pointed to faint lines on the map leading from the shoreline to the castle foundations.

"Smugglers' tunnels," Nigel confirmed. "Dating back centuries. The locals used them to move contraband up from the coves, avoiding customs officials, mostly used them for alcohol."

"Do they still exist?" Seth asked.

"I have thought about the tunnels already," Higgins began, "I sent in scouts and they reported most of the tunnels have collapsed or flooded."

"Most? But not all?" Seth asked.

"Well, according to local records, at least one passage might remain intact. It would bring us directly beneath the castle's foundations."

"It's a desperate gamble," Beth warned, her hands still working on Janssen's wounds. "If Sebastian knows about the tunnels—"

"He might not," Nathan interjected from his corner. "In all my years serving him, I never heard mention of underground passages. Sebastian avoids servant's passages too. He feels they are beneath him."

"Don't underestimate him. He may have secured these." Higgins said. "You don't get to live a long as he has without being clever enough to avoid being staked. Secret passages from the outside seem like an obvious place to seal up to me."

"Not if he doesn't know about them." Nathan replied.

Seth studied the map, tracing where the tunnel's path might be with his finger. "This is our way in."

"We'll need to scout it first," Higgins cautioned. "And even if it's passable, we're still outnumbered."

"Numbers won't matter if we strike at the right moment," Seth said. "During the day when the lesser vampires will not be out, or better yet, during the ritual, Sebastian will be vulnerable. All his focus will be on the Ascension."

"It might work." Higgins agreed. "I say again. if there is a clear tunnel. I'll send another scout to find out." He left the group and exited the cottage. He returned a moment later. "It's done."

"Good," Beth said. "I think Janssen is going to make it. help me get him into one of the rooms into a bed."

That night, Seth collapsed onto his cot in the cottage's small back room. Exhaustion pulled at him, but sleep remained elusive. He stared at the ceiling, listening to the rain. He would get to her in three days. Would she still be Emily by then? Or would Sebastian have already transformed her beyond recognition?

Sleep finally claimed him near dawn. But instead of darkness, Seth found himself in a dream, at least he thought it was a dream. He was standing in a circular stone chamber. In the center stood a stone altar, and upon it lay Emily.

She wasn't bound, yet she didn't move. Her skin had taken on a translucent quality, blue veins visible beneath the surface. Her eyes were open but unfocused, staring at nothing.

Sebastian bent over her, one wrist slashed open, dark blood dripping into Emily's parted lips. With his other hand, he pressed a silver chalice to a wound in her neck, collecting her blood.

"Drop by drop," Sebastian murmured, his voice carrying an almost religious reverence. "Your humanity fades, replaced by my essence. The perfect vessel for the Ascension."

Emily's body convulsed as Sebastian's blood entered her system. Her back arched, a silent scream frozen on her face. Seth tried to move, to reach her, but he found himself paralyzed and forced to watch.

Sebastian set down the chalice and stroked Emily's hair with terrible tenderness. "Soon you'll forget him completely. Seth will be nothing but a distant dream, a story you once heard."

Seth struggled against the invisible bonds holding him in place. Rage burned through him, hot and clarifying. This wasn't just about stopping a ritual anymore. This was about saving Emily from a fate worse than death. He had to stop her from becoming like the monster who tormented her.

He woke with a strangled cry, sweat soaking through his pajamas despite the room's chill. The vision had been so vivid, so real. It *was* a dream, right. Maybe it wasn't a dream but a connection. Despite Sebastian's efforts to sever their link, maybe something of Emily had reached out to him. He hoped that might be the case.

Chapter 17
Betrayal and Redemption

Seth studied the map on the table hoping the scout would return soon with news that one tunnel remained partially intact. It was their best hope for infiltrating the castle. He didn't have to wait too long as there was a soft knock on the door. Higgins opened it to his scout, Davies. He entered the room, and Beth brought him a cup of coffee.

"Well?" Higgins asked after the scout had taken a sip."

"It's passable. I found one of the tunnels intact." Davies said.

"That's wonderful news." Connie said.

Seth had been watching him and noticed something odd about Davies. He knew the man was one of the Society's newer members. His movements seemed mechanical, his eyes never quite focusing on anyone directly.

"Davies, pass me that journal," Higgins requested, pointing to Sebastian's leather-bound book.

Davies hesitated, his fingers lingering too long on the cover. Seth felt a strange prickling sensation at the base of his skull, the same feeling he'd experienced when touching Sebastian's journal. Without thinking, he reached out with his mind, pushing past normal perception.

The world around Davies seemed to warp, revealing a dark aura around him. Tendrils of shadow connected him to something distant, something hungry.

"Stop!" Seth lunged across the table, knocking the journal from Davies' hands. "He's compromised!"

Davies' face contorted, his features shifting from confusion to rage in an instant. "You know nothing, biographer."

"Seth, what are you—" Connie began, but fell silent as Davies pulled a ceremonial dagger from beneath his jacket.

"Sebastian sends his regards," Davies snarled, his voice suddenly carrying the same resonant quality as the vampire's. "He's quite impressed with your little rescue attempt."

Higgins moved with surprising speed for his age, positioning himself between Davies and the others. "How long have you been his pawn?"

"Longer than you've been hunting him," Davies laughed, the sound hollow and wrong. "Parts of the Society have served the elder vampires for generations. Did you really think Sebastian wouldn't have allies within our precious organization?"

Seth felt something building inside him like a pressure behind his eyes, or a buzzing in his ears. The room's edges blurred as his perception shifted again, deeper this time. He could see beyond Davies' physical form to the corruption beneath. A darkness had hollowed him out, replacing his humanity with something ancient and malevolent.

"Who else?" Seth demanded, blood beginning to trickle from his nose. "Who else belongs to him?"

Davies smiled, revealing teeth that seemed too sharp. "You'll never know until it's too late. The Society has been compromised for decades. Sebastian has eyes and ears everywhere, and he's not the only one!"

Seth pushed harder, trying to follow the dark tendrils connecting Davies to his master. Pain lanced through his skull, but he persisted, desperate to understand the extent of Sebastian's influence.

The cottage walls seemed to dissolve around him as his consciousness expanded beyond physical limitations. He could see the connections before him now like a web of dark energy stretching from Davies to the castle on the cliff, and beyond that, to other points scattered across the globe. Sebastian's network was vast, his influence reaching further than any of them had imagined.

"Seth, stop!" Connie's voice sounded distant, underwater. "You're killing yourself!"

He couldn't stop. The knowledge was there, just beyond his grasp. If he could just push a little harder, see a little deeper...

Something inside Seth's mind snapped. Blood poured from his nose and ears as he collapsed to the floor, convulsing. Through the haze of pain, he saw Davies break free from Higgins' grip, slashing wildly with the dagger before bolting for the door.

"After him!" Beth shouted, but Davies had already disappeared into the night.

Seth lay gasping on the floor, the cottage spinning around him. Connie pressed a cloth to his face, her expression tight with worry.

"The traitor," Seth managed, his voice barely audible. "He's gone."

"Don't speak," Higgins knelt beside him, checking his pulse. "We can't let you use your abilities so haphazardly anymore. You don't know what you're doing and it's irresponsible of us to allow you to continue. You can either stop being so careless, or I can perform the ritual again and close you off leaving you as you were before. You need to rest."

"No, don't do that. I need to have these abilities to defeat him." Seth struggled to sit up. "Sebastian knows everything. Our plans, our location. Davies wasn't working alone. If there really is a clear path through the tunnels, Sabastian knows about it now."

"Not if Davies never scouted them. I will send another scout."

"How can you trust another scout?" Seth asked.

Higgins exchanged grim looks with Beth and Nigel. "From now on, no one but the five of us stays in this cottage during planning. No exceptions."

"What about Nathan?" Connie asked, glancing toward the former servant who stood silently in the corner.

"I understand," Nathan said before Higgins could respond. "I served him too long. The taint never fully leaves." He gathered his few belongings. "I wish you luck. You'll need it."

After Nathan departed, Higgins turned to Seth, who still struggled to control his breathing. "Remember what I told you about symbols, Seth. Words have power, especially for creatures like Sebastian who feed off the misery of others."

Seth raised his head. "Of course. Why didn't I think of that? The biography."

"Yes," Higgins nodded. "But not the one Sebastian expects."

Despite his weakness, Seth dragged himself to the desk in the corner. "I'll write him a biography alright. One filled with every poisonous trait of his I can think of and maybe a few I can only imagine."

Seth's fingers cramped as he finished another page of the biography. Unexpectedly, each lie about Sebastian burned like acid in his veins. It had to be a physical manifestation of the connection between biographer and subject. The pain was worth it. Every falsehood weakened Sebastian's hold on reality, poisoning the narrative he'd spent centuries crafting. No, The seventh biography would not conform to the narrative Sabastian demanded of him. It would corrupt the vampire's ritual of ascension if he tried to use it.

A knock at the cottage door made everyone freeze. After Davies' betrayal, paranoia had settled over their small group like a shroud.

"I'll get it," Connie whispered, drawing a silver dagger from her boot.

Seth set down his pen, reaching for the iron fireplace poker beside his chair. His head still throbbed from his earlier collapse, but he'd recovered enough to defend himself if necessary.

Connie peered through a crack in the curtains, then stumbled back as if struck. "It can't be..."

"Who is it?" Higgins demanded, cautiously moving to her side.

Connie chuckled, "Someone very unexpected." She swung open the door. Seth's heart stopped.

Faith stood in the doorway, rain plastering her blonde hair to her face, her leather jacket gleaming with moisture. She looked exactly as she had the night he'd broken her heart, except for the silver-hilted knife strapped to her thigh and the determined set of her jaw.

"Hello, Seth," she said, her voice steady despite the emotion in her eyes. "It's been a while."

Seth rose slowly with disbelief and utter confusion. "Faith? What the hell are you doing here? How did you even find us?"

She stepped inside, closing the door against the howling wind. "The Rose and Raven Society isn't the only group tracking Sebastian Wolfram."

"You're with them?" Higgins asked sharply. "The White Covenant?"

Faith nodded. "For about three months now. Right after you and I..." She glanced at Seth, leaving the sentence unfinished.

Seth shook his head, "What? Who the hell is the White Covenant?

Higgins groaned, "Self-proclaimed white witches who do what we do, for the most part. However, their methods and ideology is somewhat different than ours."

"Faith you have been recruited by another supernatural organization. Did you know about this world while we were together?"

"Yes, I was and yeah, I did. I just never thought I would see the day when you would enter it, though."

"Why are you here?" he asked.

"To warn you." Faith shrugged off her wet jacket, revealing more weapons strapped across her body. "Your plan won't work, and you're being manipulated by people who don't have your best interests at heart."

Higgins bristled. "The Rose and Raven Society has fought creatures like Sebastian for centuries."

"And failed spectacularly," Faith countered. "How many vampires have you actually destroyed? How many rituals have you prevented?"

"More than I could ever count." Higgins said.

"Hmm. well, the White Covenant has a different approach," Faith continued. "We believe Sebastian must complete the ritual not stop it."

"What?" Seth exploded. "He's turning Emily into a monster! He's planning to resurrect some ancient evil!"

"Mortus the Ravager," Faith nodded. "We know. And we want him to succeed."

Connie stepped forward, knife still in hand. "You want Sebastian to become some kind of vampire demigod? Are you insane?"

"Not insane. Practical." Faith met Seth's gaze directly. "Mortus possesses knowledge we need. Specifically, we believe he might know how to destroy all vampires permanently. Not just stake them or burn them but eradicate their entire species from existence."

Seth stared at her, trying to reconcile this new Faith with the dance instructor he'd dated for two years. "So you're willing to sacrifice Emily? To sacrifice me?"

Faith's expression softened slightly. "I came all this way to warn you, didn't I? the White Covenant sees you as a necessary sacrifice for the greater good. I... disagree."

"You came all the way to England just to warn me?" Seth asked, genuinely surprised.

"Of course I did." Faith's voice cracked slightly revealing her true feelings for only a moment. "Just because you fell for someone else doesn't mean I stopped caring about you."

The room fell silent as everyone processed this new complication. Seth studied Faith's face, looking for deception but finding only determination and what appeared to be genuine concern.

"This changes everything," Higgins muttered. "If the White Covenant is involved..."

"It changes nothing," Seth said firmly. "I'm still saving Emily. I'm still stopping Sebastian."

"You don't understand," Faith insisted. "The White Covenant has infiltrated the Society even more deeply than Sebastian has. Half your team probably reports to them."

"When we return to headquarters, I think it's time for a thorough house cleaning!" Higgins said.

Beth and Nigel exchanged uncomfortable glances.

"Is that true?" Seth demanded. "Do you two report to the White Covenant?"

Neither answered immediately.

"Jesus," Seth began, "Does anyone actually want to stop this ritual?"

"I do," Connie stepped to his side. "Emily doesn't deserve this fate, regardless of what knowledge Mortus might possess."

Seth felt a surge of gratitude toward her. At least someone still had their priorities straight.

"No, we are not part of the White Covenant." Beth said finally, "but we do agree with Faith if they are truly seeking to destroy all vampires."

"Yes, we have come across the same information about Mortus." Nigel added.

"So what now?" Seth asked, looking around the fractured group. "We just split into factions and work against each other?"

"That appears to be the case," Higgins said regretfully. "I'm sorry, Seth, but the Society's primary mission has always been knowledge. If there's a chance to learn how to eradicate vampires permanently..."

"Then you're no better than Sebastian," Seth finished. "Using people as tools for your own ends."

Faith stepped closer to Seth. "Come with me. The White Covenant can protect you, at least."

"I'm not going anywhere," Seth replied. "Not without Emily."

Faith nodded, as if she'd expected this answer. "Then I'll stay and help you. My mission was to bring you in, but..." She shrugged. "I've never been great at following orders."

Seth closed his eyes, reaching out through his connection to Emily. For days it had been blocked, but now, as his abilities grew stronger, he felt something, a flicker of consciousness, like a candle flame in darkness.

Emily? he called silently.

To his shock, she answered. *Seth? I can hear you!*

Her mental voice sounded different—sharper, more focused, yet somehow fragmented, as if parts of her were speaking from different places simultaneously.

I'm coming for you, he promised. *Hold on.*

It's too late, she replied. *I'm changing. I can feel both worlds now human and vampire. It's... extraordinary. Look, I can talk to you this way now. It wasn't even a possibility before."*

Fight it! Seth urged.

No, listen! Emily's mental voice grew stronger. *This is an advantage. I can see his plans now. The ritual, the manuscripts, everything. He doesn't realize I can access his thoughts when he feeds on me.*

Seth's stomach turned at the image, but he forced himself to focus. *What is he planning?*

The ritual requires seven biographers, seven manuscripts. But there's something he's hiding from everyone—the resurrection isn't just about power. Mortus is his maker's maker, the progenitor of his bloodline. Sebastian believes Mortus can free him from his vampiric nature entirely.

Make him human again? Seth asked, incredulously.

No. Something else. Something beyond both human and vampire. And Seth, her voice began to fade. *He knows you're coming. The tunnels are trapped. Don't—*

The connection severed abruptly, leaving Seth gasping.

"What is it?" Connie asked, steadying him.

"Emily," Seth managed. "I reached her. She's changing, existing in both states—human and vampire. She can see Sebastian's plans."

"That's impossible," Higgins said. "The transformation doesn't work that way."

"Nothing about this situation follows the rules," Faith pointed out. "What did she say?"

Seth looked around the room, making a split-second decision about who to trust. "Connie, Faith—we need to talk. Alone."

Chapter 18
Between Worlds

Seth led Faith and Connie to the small back room of the cottage, closing the door behind them. The space felt claustrophobic with three people, but it was the only place they could speak without being overheard. He leaned against the wall.

"No Higgins?" Connie asked.

"Not with that statement of going through with the ritual."

"I said that too." Faith said.

Seth shook his head, "Never mind that for now. I'm sure Connie will fill him in later. What I want to talk about is Emily. She's in transition," he explained, keeping his voice low. "She's not fully vampire yet, but she's not human either. She exists in both worlds simultaneously."

"That's why you can still reach her," Connie realized. "Your connection bridges the gap between states."

Faith crossed her arms. "What else did she tell you?"

"Not a lot. Since the connection now flows in both directions, I am expecting her to make contact with me at any second. She told me she would when she had a moment away from the bastard."

Connie took a deep breath, "All right, you need to see if you can get her to tell you a few things we have to know to infiltrate the castle. Also, and I hesitate to mention it, but she betrayed you and left you for Sabastian...willingly. She already knew what he was and she did it anyway. How can you trust her now. What has changed?"

"He has fed on her! He has taken her by force. I saw it. No one would put up with that."

Faith spoke up, "I know you don't want to hear from me on this subject, but yes, she would put up with it. It actually turns on some people. I have been studying the situation with other vampire to human couples and there is a form of ecstasy that comes from the feeding. Since he is a psychic vampire as well, he can feed off your misery, but he can also take her misery away."

"Ah, but he will stop short of making her happy. Those emotions would hurt him." Seth pointed out.

"You have me there." Faith said.

As they continued to speak, Seth noticed the room around him began to shift. The walls seemed to breathe, expanding and contracting like lungs. Seth blinked hard, but the distortion remained.

"Seth?" Connie's voice sounded distant. "What's wrong?"

He couldn't answer. His perception had split, like looking through a prism. The cottage remained visible, but overlaid upon it was... something else. A vast, swirling darkness punctuated by points of cold light. Not star, but something alive and aware. Watching.

"I can see it," he whispered, transfixed. "The boundary between worlds. It's here, between worlds, where Mortus waits."

Faith grabbed his shoulders. "Seth, focus on my voice. Come back."

But he couldn't look away from the darkness. Within it shapes moved and writhed; ancient, terrible things that had never known human form. And among them, a presence that radiated malevolence so profound it made Sebastian seem benign by comparison.

Seth. Emily's voice cut through the vision, clearer than before. *Can you see me?*

He searched the darkness until he found her. She was a figure of light and shadow, neither fully here nor there. Parts of her flickered between human and something else, her form unstable but her eyes unmistakably Emily's.

I see you, he replied, relief washing through him despite the horror of their surroundings.

Sebastian doesn't know I can reach this place consciously, she explained. *He thinks I'm just a vessel, but the transformation has given me access to both realms.*

What is this place? Seth asked, struggling to maintain his focus as the darkness closed in around them.

The threshold. Where beings like Mortus exist when they're not manifested in our world. Emily's form wavered. *Sebastian has collected blood from all six previous biographers. Their man-*

uscripts form a circle in the ritual chamber. Yours is the final piece—the keystone that completes the magical circuit.

But I haven't finished it, Seth protested.

He doesn't need you to finish it. He just needs your blood and creative essence to complete the set. Emily's expression grew urgent. *The eclipse is tomorrow night. Once it begins, he'll open the gateway whether you're there physically or not.*

If he doesn't need me physically, then why does he keep me alive?

"*I thought that would be obvious. He is getting too much from your constant worry and misery to let you go just yet. He enjoys tormenting you.*

The darkness around them surged suddenly, as if responding to their conversation. A presence approached, an ancient, hungry, monstrous, and aware beast. Seth felt it reaching for him, probing his consciousness with cold tendrils of thought.

He knows you're here, Emily warned. *Mortus senses you. Go back, now!*

Seth tried to withdraw, but the darkness clung to him like tar. The presence drew closer, its attention fixed on him with terrible intensity.

Why the hell did you bring me here to this place, Emily? Connie's concerns of her loyalty was in the forefront of his thoughts. Was Emily baiting him?

SETH! Emily screamed, her form lunging forward to push him away.

He crashed back into his body with such force that he collapsed to the floor. Faith and Connie were kneeling beside him with fear prominent in their worried expressions. He became aware of the blood once again streaming from his nose and ears.

"Get Higgins," Faith ordered, and Connie rushed from the room.

"What happened?" Faith demanded, helping Seth sit up.

"I saw... beyond," he managed, his voice raw. "The place where Mortus waits. Emily's there, caught between worlds."

Higgins burst into the room, his face grim. "If you keep bleeding out like this it won't matter how your abilities are manifesting. You will be dead from blood loss!" He turned his attention to Connie, "It's an official order now. Use whatever gift you have to stop him from astral projecting."

Connie breathed in deeply, "Sorry kid, but you heard him. I have the ability to keep you in your body and I have to obey that order. No more roaming the realms."

"I don't have time for training or for Connie to babysit me," Seth gasped. "The eclipse is tomorrow night."

"Then we need to stabilize you, at least temporarily." Higgins knelt beside him, examining the blood still flowing from Seth's nose. "I can perform another ritual."

"No, you want to return me to the way I was before."

"This ritual is Just a stopgap measure to prevent further deterioration. You will keep your abilities, but they won't keep ravaging your body this way, at least not for the time being."

"Do it," Seth agreed.

"You understand this is only temporary?" Higgins warned. "Eventually, these powers will overwhelm you again without proper guidance."

Seth thought of Emily, caught between worlds, fighting alone. "I don't care. I need to be functional."

Higgins nodded grimly. "Very well. Faith, Connie, help me prepare."

Seth watched Faith from across the cottage's main room as she spread a detailed map of the castle across the table, her face set in concentration. It still felt surreal seeing her here, fighting alongside him after everything that had happened between them.

"The ritual chamber is here," Faith said, tapping a circular room in the castle's north tower. "Sebastian's quarters connect directly to it through this passage."

Higgins nodded, making notes in his journal. "And the defenses?"

"Human guards patrol the main entrances. Lesser vampires roam the interior corridors." Faith's gaze flicked briefly to Seth. "But the tunnels... Sebastian believes now that they're too obvious an approach. He's set traps, but minimal personnel."

Seth moved closer, studying the map. "So he thinks we wouldn't dare use them because we'd assume they're heavily guarded?"

"Exactly." Faith's lips curved into a half-smile. "Classic misdirection. Since he is aware of the them now, and he made sure that we knew he was, he's expecting us to try something more elaborate."

Seth couldn't help wondering what had happened during that meeting between Higgins, Connie, and the White Covenant representatives. They'd disappeared for hours, returning with Faith in tow and the announcement that the White Covenant had agreed to withdraw from the case. Faith had been officially "released" to join them, though she made it clear her allegiance was to Emily's rescue, and not to Rose and Raven Society protocols.

"What did you say to them?" Seth had asked Higgins privately.

"Let's just say we reached an understanding about mutual interests," Higgins had replied cryptically. "Some battles aren't worth fighting on multiple fronts."

Now, watching Faith work with them as if she'd always been part of the team, Seth felt a complicated tangle of emotions. The hurt of their breakup had faded, replaced by something like respect. She'd come all this way to warn him, after all. That had to mean something.

"You're staring," Faith said without looking up from the map.

"Sorry." Seth moved to her side. "Just... processing all this."

Faith straightened, meeting his eyes directly. "Look, I know this is weird. Us working together after everything."

"It's fine," Seth said quickly. "We're adults. We can be professional."

"Professional." Faith's mouth quirked. "Is that what we're calling hunting vampires now?"

Despite everything, Seth laughed. It felt good, that momentary release of tension. Faith laughed too, and for a second, it was like before, before Emily, before Sebastian, before their relationship had fractured beyond repair.

"I never hated you," Faith said quietly when their laughter subsided. "I was hurt, but I understood. Sometimes things just... end."

"I never wanted to hurt you," Seth replied, meaning it. "You deserved better."

"Maybe." Faith shrugged. "Or maybe we just weren't right for each other. It doesn't mean I stopped caring about what happens to you."

The admission warmed his heart. Maybe, when all this was over, if they both survived... He pushed the thought away. Emily needed him now. There would be time for sorting out his complicated feelings later.

"We should move at midnight," Higgins announced, breaking their moment. "The eclipse begins at 3 AM. That gives us three hours to reach the ritual chamber."

Seth nodded, pulling his manuscript from his bag. He'd been working on it steadily, filling pages with carefully crafted words designed to undermine Sebastian's power. The connection between biographer and subject worked both ways. If Sebastian could draw power from Seth's writing, then perhaps Seth could use that same connection as a weapon. It sounded good to him, anyway. Whether it would work or not was an entirely different matter.

"I've been experimenting," Seth explained, showing them a passage he'd written. "When I write certain words, I can feel Sebastian's reaction. It's like... disrupting a frequency."

'Words have power!" Higgins said, smiling at him.

Connie leaned over his shoulder. "Yes, Words have power. Especially for creatures that feed on creative energy."

"Exactly." Seth flipped through the pages. "I've identified key phrases that seem particularly effective. If I write them at strategic moments during our approach..."

"You could create windows of opportunity," Faith finished, impressed. "Temporary weaknesses in his defenses."

Seth nodded. "That's the theory, anyway."

As the others finalized their preparations, Seth closed his eyes, reaching cautiously for his connection to Emily. Since Higgins' stabilizing ritual, he could maintain the link without hemorrhaging, though Connie's presence kept him firmly anchored in his body.

Emily's consciousness felt different now—sharper, more diffuse, existing in multiple places simultaneously. The transformation was nearly complete. She was becoming something neither fully human nor fully vampire, but something unique, straddling both worlds.

Emily? he called softly.

Seth. Her response came immediately, her mental voice resonating with new harmonics. *You're coming tonight.*

Yes. Can you hold on until we reach you?

A pause. *I'm not sure I need rescuing anymore.*

Seth's heart stuttered. *What do you mean?*

This transformation... it's not what Sebastian intended. I can see things now, Seth. Feel things. The power is... intoxicating.

Emily, he's using you for the ritual. You're in danger.

Am I? Her mental voice carried a note of genuine curiosity. *Or am I becoming something beyond his control?*

Seth opened his eyes, cold dread settling in his stomach. What if they were too late? What if Emily couldn't be restored to her former self? What if she didn't want to be? Was she using him all along? He decided it was best not to inform the others of what he had just learned. It might have a negative effect on the mission.

Chapter 19
The Seventh Manuscript

Seth followed the narrow tunnel, his footsteps muffled by centuries of accumulated dust. The ancient stone walls pressed in around him, slick with moisture that seeped through cracks in the mortar. His flashlight beam cut through darkness that felt almost alive, revealing cobwebs and the occasional scurrying creature disturbed by his presence.

The team had separated twenty minutes ago at a junction where the smugglers' passage split into three branches. Connie and Higgins had taken the left fork, heading toward the outer perimeter of the ritual site where they would disrupt Sebastian's protective circles. Faith, Nigel, and Beth had gone right, planning to create enough chaos to draw attention away from the center.

Which left Seth alone, following the middle path directly toward the heart of Sebastian's domain. He was surprised they allowed him to go off on his own, but he didn't question it too much.

His manuscript was safely tucked away inside his backpack, each page carefully crafted to undermine the vampire's power. Seth had written through the night, pouring everything he'd learned about Sebastian into words designed to wound rather than flatter. If his theory was correct, the connection between biographer and subject could be weaponized. Sabastian might have an unpleasant surprise when he used *this* manuscript in the ritual.

The tunnel widened, opening into an ancient crypt. Seth's flashlight revealed stone niches carved into the walls, but instead of the expected skeletal remains, he found something far more disturbing.

"My God," he whispered, his voice echoing in the chamber.

Six bodies sat upright in the niches, perfectly preserved yet unmistakably dead. Their skin had the texture of ancient parchment, pulled tight over bone. Each clutched a manuscript to their chest, pages yellowed with age but somehow intact. Their eyes were open, staring sightlessly forward, expressions frozen in what looked like rapture or agony, or perhaps both.

Seth approached the nearest figure, a woman in clothing that appeared to be from the 1950s. Her manuscript's title page read "Sebastian: Immortal Visionary" in elegant script. The author's name, Agatha Martin, matched one of the journals Seth had found in Sebastian's hidden compartment.

"He kept you," Seth murmured, horror and pity washing through him. "All of you."

These were Sebastian's previous biographers. They were not buried or disposed of as Seth had assumed, but preserved here, their creative essence somehow still powering Sebastian's magic. He could feel it now, a low vibration of energy emanating from each corpse feeding into the stone beneath his feet.

None of the accounts he'd found in Sebastian's apartment had mentioned this. Nothing had prepared him for the reality that these writers hadn't just died. He had no idea they'd been transformed into batteries, their life force continuously drained to fuel Sebastian's immortality. But then again, why would Sabastian want to let him, another biographer he planned to use, know about such a thing?

Seth forced himself to continue past the macabre display, following a narrow staircase that spiraled downward. The air grew colder with each step, carrying the metallic scent of blood and something else that smelled like ozone, or like the air before a lightning strike.

The staircase ended at a massive iron door, its surface covered in symbols that hurt Seth's eyes to look at directly. Symbols of power like Higgins was always reminding him. Only these symbols were against him this time. He placed his hand against the cold metal, feeling the vibrations of power beyond. Keeping his eyes closed so he didn't have to see the symbols and taking a deep breath, he pushed.

The door swung open silently, revealing a vast circular chamber carved from the rock beneath the castle. Six ornate writing desks formed a perfect hexagon around a central altar where

Emily lay motionless, her skin pale as moonlight. She writhed back and forth, seemingly unaware of her surroundings or him for that matter. Crystal structures rose from the floor around her, filled with stolen life force that flowed with tiny ghostly figures inside whose forms he couldn't quite make out through channels carved into the stone.

Sebastian stood before a seventh desk, more elaborate than the others, positioned directly opposite the entrance. He didn't turn as Seth entered, but his voice carried clearly across the chamber.

"Welcome, Chronicler," Sebastian said, his tone almost warm. "I knew you'd come. Your desk awaits."

Seth stepped fully into the room, the iron door swinging shut behind him with a final-sounding thud. Emily's eyes were open but unfocused. She was still now, her chest barely moving with shallow breaths. Tubes of plastic flowing up to the crystal connected her to the structure, carrying what looked like blood, both hers and Sebastian's, in a continuous circuit.

"What have you done to her?" Seth demanded, his voice echoing in the vast space.

Sebastian turned then, his face serene, almost beautiful in the low light. He wore ceremonial robes of a deep shade of crimson, embroidered with the same symbols that adorned the door. "Don't you already know? I've elevated her," he replied. "Given her a glimpse of what awaits us all."

"You've been lying from the beginning," Seth said, taking a cautious step forward. "This was never about your biography, not a publishable one at least."

Sebastian smiled, his teeth gleaming unnaturally white in the dim light. "Oh, but it was. Just not in the way you imagined." He gestured to the seventh desk, its surface pristine, waiting. "Your predecessors wrote their parts. Now it's your turn to complete the circle."

"And if I refuse?"

"Look at her, Seth." Sebastian moved to Emily's side, brushing a strand of hair from her face with disturbing tenderness. "She exists in two states simultaneously. Human and vampire, life and death, balanced on the edge of a knife." His fingers traced the tubes connecting her to the crystal structures. "That balance cannot hold. Without the completed ritual, the transformation will tear her apart from within."

Seth's stomach twisted as Emily's body suddenly convulsed, her back arching off the altar. A strangled sound escaped her lips. The sound was not quite a scream, and it was not quite a moan. It was a sickening growl.

"What's happening to her?" Seth demanded, rushing forward only to be stopped by an invisible barrier a few feet from the altar.

"The eclipse begins," Sebastian said, glancing upward through the skylight fixed into the stone ceiling. "Her time runs short, as does yours."

Outside the ritual chamber, Faith moved silently through the castle corridors. In spite of their more advanced age, Beth and Nigel followed close behind. They'd encountered minimal resistance just as Faith had predicted, Sebastian had concentrated his forces elsewhere, expecting them to execute a different approach.

"The north tower should be just ahead," Faith whispered, checking the hand-drawn map one last time before tucking it away.

A scream echoed from somewhere above them, followed by the sound of breaking glass. Faith froze, signaling the others to do the same. Footsteps pounded overhead, then silence.

"That didn't sound like Seth or Emily," Beth murmured.

"No," Faith agreed. "Higgins and Connie must have run into trouble."

Several floors above, Higgins pressed himself against a wall as a lesser vampire lunged past him, its movements jerky and uncoordinated but it was terrifyingly fast. Connie swung a silver-bladed machete, catching the creature across its shoulder. It howled, black ichor spraying from the wound.

"The coffin has to be here somewhere," Higgins gasped, scanning the opulent bedroom they'd broken into. "Check under the floorboards!"

Connie ducked another attack, rolling beneath an antique table. "Kind of busy at the moment!"

Two more vampires burst through the doorway, their faces twisted in hunger and rage. Unlike Sebastian's elegant control, these lesser creatures were little more than animated corpses, driven by bloodlust and their master's will.

"We need to hurry," Higgins said, pulling a vial of consecrated oil from his pocket. "The eclipse has begun."

"What are we doing up here in the vampire's bedchamber anyway. Wouldn't his coffin be down the basement somewhere."

"You have been watching too many vampire movies. They almost never keep their important coffins exactly where you think they would. Especially not low and vulnerable in a basement where every single vampire cliche' movie would suggest they'd be kept."

"Sorry, I was just speculating." She dodged another lesser vampire attack.

In the ritual chamber, Seth felt the change in the air as the moon began to darken. The crystals surrounding Emily shone with increasing intensity, the ghostly figures within them becoming more agitated, more distinct.

"What do you really want?" Seth asked, his eyes fixed on Emily's suffering form.

Sebastian's expression shifted, becoming almost wistful. "Freedom. The same thing I've wanted for centuries." He moved to the seventh desk, running his long fingernail along its polished surface. "Mortus can grant that. Oh, not for just me, but to all of our kind. No more hunger, no more… limitations."

"At what cost?"

"A new world order, certainly." Sebastian shrugged as if discussing a minor political realignment rather than global catastrophe. "Humans would serve rather than rule. But is that truly so different from how things already are? The powerful have always fed on the weak."

"That's insane!" Seth's gaze returned to Emily as she convulsed again, more violently this time. Blood trickled from her nose, her ears, her eyes, just as it had from Seth when his abilities overwhelmed him.

"Here is my offer," Sebastian said, his voice dropping to a silky whisper. "Take your place at the desk. Complete the manuscript. You must do it willingly of your own hand. Do this, and Emily goes free. Her transformation will stabilize, and she will live."

"And if I refuse?"

"Again you ask that. If you refuse, then watch as she is torn apart from within." Sebastian's face hardened. "Look, I'm going to begin the ritual whether you comply or not. If you still refuse, the ritual will collapse, and with it, any chance of saving her."

Seth looked from Emily to the waiting desk, understanding at last the true horror of Sebastian's plan. The vampire had never intended to merely feed on his suffering or kill him like the others. As a man now open to the forces of the unknown through the same ritual that gave him his abilities, Seth was the perfect vessel to host Mortus' resurrection.

"You need me to write it willingly," Seth realized. "That's why you kept me alive, why you orchestrated all of this."

"The seventh manuscript must be completed by your hand, freely given," Sebastian confirmed. "Only then can the circle be complete."

"But if you force me to complete it by this impossible choice, that's not completing it freely of my own hand."

"You're stalling by posing semantics. If you complete the manuscript by making a choice to do so, that counts as freely writing it by your own hand and by your own choice. You have the ability to make a different choice."

"Yeah, one with the same horrible outcome."

"Nevertheless, I suggest you make your choice quickly if you want Emily's suffering to be minimal. Once I begin the ritual and you do not comply causing it to collapse, she will die in agony in seconds."

Outside, the moon continued its inexorable slide into shadow. Emily's body jerked and twisted on the altar. Seth hesitated.

"Choose, Seth," Sebastian urged, you have seconds. When the moon is completely covered, I will begin the ritual. "Her life, or your principles. The clock is ticking."

A terrible thought invaded his mind. What if Emily was still with Sabastian and she wanted to become a vampire. She so much as told him so earlier. Something didn't add up with her. She had already made him into a fool once when she left him for Sabastian. what if this was all part of the elaborate plan?

"I...I need your word and reassurance this isn't some kind of elaborate ruse. Let her go first, and once I know she is safe and everything is on the up and up, I'll help you finish the ritual."

"Nope, sorry Seth. You have waited too long." He raised his arm above his head with a ceremonial dagger in hand. With that gesture, he had begun the ritual.

Chapter 20
Shadow of the Eclipse

Seth slumped his shoulders in defeat and moved toward the seventh desk. The ancient wood gleamed in the eerie light, its surface unmarked save for a single quill pen resting in a silver holder.

"A wise decision," Sebastian purred, approaching with a roll of yellowed parchment. "This paper has absorbed the blood of a thousand victims over the centuries. The perfect medium for our final chronicle."

Seth unrolled the parchment, his fingers trembling. The material felt wrong against his skin, not quite paper, not quite leather, but something unsettlingly in between. Sebastian placed the quill in his hand. The nib pricked Seth's finger, drawing a bead of blood that flowed up the shaft and into the reservoir.

"Your own blood will serve as ink," Sebastian explained. "The connection must be direct."

Around the chamber, the air shimmered as Sebastian began a guttural chant in a language Seth didn't recognize. The words seemed to bend reality, creating ripples in the air that connected all seven desks. At each of the other six stations, translucent figures materialized, they had to be the previous biographers, their faces frozen in expressions of perpetual horror.

Morrison sat at the desk directly across from Seth, his ghostly hands moving across phantom pages. Chen worked to his right, eyes vacant yet somehow aware. Four others Seth didn't recognize completed the circle, all trapped in an endless cycle of creation, their creative essence feeding Sebastian's ritual even beyond death. He suddenly became aware that their fate might also be intended to become his fate.

The vampire's chanting intensified. The crystals gleamed in rhythm with his words, each surge drawing a pained gasp from Emily. Seth glanced at her, his heart twisting at the sight of blood streaming from her eyes and ears.

Seth. Her voice brushed against his mind, weaker than before but unmistakably present. *Listen carefully.*

He bent over the parchment, pretending to contemplate his first words while focusing on Emily's faint mental voice.

He made a mistake. Each word seemed to cost her tremendous effort. *The ritual... requires truth... but truth is... subjective.*

Seth understood immediately. Sebastian needed him to write willingly, but the vampire had never specified what he must write. The fool just assumed he would comply and write something flattering like he had seen on the title of the manuscript the woman in the crypt held earlier. The ritual required the seventh manuscript to complete the magical circuit, but perhaps the content mattered more than Sebastian realized.

Higgins' words echoed in his memory: "Words have power. Symbols on paper are just that...symbols you have trained your brain to interpret."

Seth dipped the quill in the small pool of blood that had formed on his fingertip and began to write. The script flowed easily, elegant phrases praising Sebastian's nobility, his centuries of suffering, his righteous quest for freedom. Exactly what the vampire wanted. Sabastian paused his ritualistic chants to check on the prose, to make sure Seth was writing what he wanted. He hovered for a moment, glancing over his shoulder at what he was writing. Satisfied, he returned to his chanting.

But as he wrote, Seth focused on the techniques Higgins had taught him during their brief training. He used his ability to layer meaning into text, to create words that carried dual purposes. With each stroke of the quill, he infused a second narrative beneath the first, visible only to those with the sight to perceive it.

This hidden text told a different story—Sebastian's cruelty, his manipulation, the hollow emptiness at his core. Seth wrote of the vampire's fear, his weakness, his fundamental inability to ever achieve the transcendence he sought. Each word was a poison pill wrapped in the candy-coating Sebastian craved.

The vampire moved behind him once more, perhaps sensing something might be wrong. He read over his shoulder. Seth froze for a brief moment. Sabastian had better only see the text praising him or he was a dead man now rather than later.

"Excellent," Sabastian murmured. "Continue."

Seth began writing again. He felt Sebastian's cold presence at his back, but the vampire saw only what he wanted to see, which was the surface narrative that stroked his ego and supported his delusions. The deeper text remained invisible to him, a secret weapon taking shape with every word.

As Seth wrote, something unexpected happened. A giddiness bloomed in his chest, not the burning rage that had driven him for weeks, but something lighter, brighter. Genuine satisfaction. Joy, even. The realization that he was outwitting the creature who had caused him so much pain and suffering filled him with authentic... happiness!

Sebastian hissed suddenly, stepping back from the desk. "What are you doing?" he demanded, his face contorting in discomfort.

"Writing your biography," he said as he continued working, the warmth within him growing stronger. He understood how the vampire's weakness worked now. Sebastian fed on misery, on suffering and despair. But true happiness, genuine joy? These emotions were toxic to him, disrupting his ability to maintain control.

That's it, Emily's voice came stronger now. *He can't stop you when you're truly happy. Keep writing.*

Seth let the feeling expand, embracing the satisfaction of turning Sebastian's own ritual against him. The vampire retreated further, his expression a mixture of confusion and growing alarm.

"Stop!" Sebastian commanded, but the ritual had already linked them. He couldn't interfere without collapsing the entire magical structure he'd spent centuries creating. The vampire launched into a panic as he lost control of the situation. "Your girlfriend. I took her from you! I had my way with her" he said in desperation.

The problem was Seth knew it was a desperate move, so he didn't let it get to him. His happiness grew with the knowledge the bastard couldn't take back control.

The ghostly biographers at the other desks seemed to sense the disruption. Their movements faltered, heads turning toward Seth as if drawn by his emotional state. For the first time, he saw awareness flicker in their vacant eyes, the faintest spark of hope. They saw what he was trying to do.

The chamber trembled as the ritual intensified. Through the skylight, Seth watched the moon's edge disappear into shadow. The eclipse was progressing faster than he'd anticipated. Around him, the air became laden with energy as the six ghostly biographers continued their endless writing, though their spectral eyes now flickered toward him with growing awareness.

A commotion echoed from somewhere below, the clash of weapons, the unmistakable sound of Faith's voice barking orders. The cavalry had arrived.

Sebastian's head snapped toward the noise. "Your friends are persistent, if not foolish." His lips curled into a sneer. "It changes nothing. The barriers will hold until the ritual is complete."

Seth kept writing, his quill never pausing. Each word strengthened the dual narrative with false praise on the surface, and abject condemnation beneath. The happiness in his chest expanded, a warm glow that seemed to physically repel Sebastian whenever the vampire approached.

A sudden explosion rocked the castle foundations. Dust rained from the ancient ceiling.

"What have they done?" Sebastian snarled, momentarily distracted.

Seth seized the opportunity, reaching out mentally to Emily. *Can you hear me?*

Yes. Her voice was stronger now, more present. *Higgins and Connie are dismantling the outer wards. I can feel the magical barriers weakening.*

Hold on. I'm almost finished with the manuscript.

Sebastian returned his attention to the ritual, his chanting growing more urgent as the moon slipped further into darkness. The crystals surged, drawing more energy from Emily. Her body convulsed on the altar. Sabastian took a dagger and went to her. "Let's see how happy this makes you?" he plunged the knife into her leg. She writhed in pain, crying out.

Seth's happiness faltered at the sight of her suffering. He needed to maintain his emotional state, it was their only advantage, but Emily's pain tore at him. An idea formed, terrible but necessary.

Setting down his quill, Seth stood abruptly.

"What are you doing?" Sebastian demanded. "The manuscript isn't complete!"

"I need to see her," Seth said, moving toward the altar.

Sebastian hesitated, then nodded. "Make it quick. The eclipse reaches totality in seconds."

Seth approached Emily, his heart breaking at her condition. Her skin had turned translucent, veins darkened with Sebastian's blood visible beneath. Her eyes, when they fluttered open, shifted between human brown and vampire amber.

"I'm sorry," Seth whispered, leaning close as if to kiss her forehead. "What was I thinking. Getting closer to you is not helping me hold on to my happiness like I thought it would," he saw the two vampire teeth marks on her neck. "Instead, it's pissing me off!"

Then out of frustration he pressed his thumb hard against the wounds on her neck.

Emily's scream pierced the chamber. Seth felt her agony as if it were his own, the connection between them amplifying the sensation. His happiness shattered, replaced by horror at what he'd done and hatred for the creature who had forced his hand. He spun around to glare at the bastard vampire.

Sebastian's posture straightened immediately, strength returning to his frame as he fed on Seth's renewed misery. "Yes," he breathed, a smug smile spreading across his face. "Now you understand your place."

Seth stumbled back to the desk, his hands shaking as he picked up the quill. The warmth that had protected him was gone, replaced by cold fury and despair. Sebastian moved closer, confidence restored, his chanting growing louder as the eclipse neared totality.

"You see? You cannot defeat me," Sebastian gloated between verses. "I have fed on greater suffering than yours for centuries."

Seth's quill trembled above the parchment. He'd lost his advantage, his protection. But as he glanced around the chamber, he noticed the ghostly biographers still watching him intently. They had seen what he'd done with the manuscript. He knew immediately when he made eye contact with each one of them. They could see the truth hidden beneath lies. They understood.

Morrison's spectral form nodded almost imperceptibly. Chen's ghost raised a translucent hand toward Seth's manuscript. The others followed suit, their attention shifting from their own writing to his.

Seth realized what was happening. They were choosing him over Sebastian. Choosing truth over the lies they'd been forced to write.

The moon disappeared completely behind Earth's shadow. The eclipse reached totality. Sebastian raised his arms triumphantly, launching into the final incantation.

"Mortus, ancient one, I call you forth! Cross the threshold between worlds and claim this vessel prepared for your return!"

The crystals flared blindingly bright. Emily's body arched off the altar, suspended in midair. Sebastian's voice rose to a fever pitch, ancient words tumbling from his lips with increasing speed.

But something was wrong. The ghostly biographers had stopped writing. One by one, their spectral forms dissolved, their essence flowing not toward the summoning crystal as Sebastian intended, but into Seth's manuscript.

"No!" Sebastian screamed, realizing too late what was happening. "Return to your stations! Complete the connection!"

Seth's manuscript began to glow with an inner light as it absorbed the freed souls of the previous writers. The dual narrative, truth and falsehood occupying the same space, created a paradox in the magical circuit, a contradiction that the ritual couldn't resolve.

He felt momentary happiness again then he fixed his eyes on Emily in a panic. He had forgotten what Sabastian had said the collapse of the ritual would do to her. He ran to her and yanked the tubes from her body and lifted her off the stone alter and held her close while willing protections to form around them. He could feel the trickle of blood running from his nose. Higgins' temporary fix had worn off. He was hemorrhaging again, but he didn't care. He held fast to Emily.

Sebastian lunged toward Seth and Emily, but an invisible barrier repelled him. The vampire's face contorted with rage and disbelief as his carefully constructed ritual collapsed around him.

"What have you done?" he howled.

Chapter 21
No More Sacrifices

The chamber shook violently as Sebastian's form began to change. His elegant features elongated, skin splitting to reveal grayish scales beneath. His jaw dislocated with a sickening crack, extending to accommodate rows of needle-like teeth that pushed through his gums in bloody profusion. Wings, not the leathery bat-like appendages of folklore but something more primordial, tore through his ceremonial robes, spreading wide in the confined space.

"You think you've won?" Sebastian's voice had transformed too, becoming a multi-toned hiss that seemed to come from everywhere at once. "I've prepared for centuries. There are contingencies you cannot imagine."

Seth clutched Emily tighter as Sebastian launched himself forward, claws extended. The attack came with such speed that

Seth barely had time to react. He stumbled backward, losing his grip on Emily as Sebastian's talons raked across his chest. Pain bloomed hot and immediate as Seth crashed against one of the writing desks, splintering ancient wood.

"The ritual will be completed," Sebastian snarled, advancing on Seth. "If not with your cooperation, then with your blood."

Seth scrambled backward, his hand finding the manuscript he'd written. It still glowed with the absorbed essence of the previous biographers. Sebastian loomed over him, raising clawed hands for a killing blow.

A blur of movement intercepted the vampire. Emily stood between them, her body radiating an otherworldly light. Her eyes had settled into a strange new state, making Seth do a double take.

"Enough," she said, her voice carrying new harmonics that made the air vibrate. "You've taken enough from us."

Sebastian faltered, genuine surprise crossing his monstrous features. "You cannot resist me. You are mine."

"I was never yours," Emily replied. "The transformation you forced on me didn't quite work the way you planned."

Seth stared in wonder. Emily's form seemed to flicker between states, sometimes solid, sometimes translucent. The unique transitional state Sebastian had forced upon her had created something the vampire hadn't anticipated. She had become a being who could move between worlds at will.

Sebastian's surprise gave way to rage. He threw back his head and released a howl that shook dust from the ceiling. "To me, my children! Your master calls!"

Shadows coalesced around the chamber's perimeter as lesser vampires materialized from darkness. Their forms were crude compared to Sebastian's, more corpse-like, but their numbers were concerning. At least a dozen surrounded them, hissing and snapping.

The chamber lurched sideways as another explosion rocked the castle. Cracks spread across the ancient stone ceiling, chunks of masonry crashing to the floor. The magical backlash from the interrupted ritual was destabilizing the entire structure.

"Seth!" Faith's voice cut through the chaos as she burst through a side entrance, silver blade flashing. Behind her came Higgins, Connie, and the others, weapons drawn and faces grim with determination.

The chamber erupted into battle. Faith moved with practiced efficiency, her blade finding vampire flesh with unerring accuracy. Higgins knelt in the center of the room, chalk flying across stone as he sketched a containment circle, his voice rising in urgent incantation.

"The magical energies are tearing reality apart!" Higgins shouted over the din. "I can slow it but not stop it!"

Seth watched as cracks appeared in the air itself, jagged lines of nothingness that revealed glimpses of the threshold realm he'd seen in his vision. It was the place where Mortus waited. The ritual hadn't failed completely; it had simply stalled at its most dangerous point.

A terrible moment of clarity came over Seth as he saw the realm of Mortus materializing. The power Sebastian had accumulated couldn't simply dissipate. It had to go somewhere. And right now, it was tearing apart the barrier between worlds.

"The energy," Seth gasped, struggling to his feet. "It needs a vessel."

Emily saw what he was about to attempt. He could see it in her eyes. "Seth, No!"

But he had already made his decision. Seth grabbed the glowing manuscript and pressed it against his chest. The power Sebastian had intended for Mortus' resurrection surged into him instead, a torrent of magical energy that threatened to incinerate him from within.

Pain beyond anything he'd experienced engulfed him. He felt as though he had poured gasoline over himself and struck a match. Seth fell to his knees, every cell in his body screaming as the power coursed through him. Blood poured from his eyes, his nose, his ears. Too much, it was too much for any human to contain.

Then Emily was there, her hands on his face, her forehead pressed against his. "Hold on," she whispered. "I can help."

Seth felt her consciousness merge with his, her unique state between worlds creating a bridge. She became a conduit, drawing the excess energy through herself and dispersing it safely across the threshold between realms. The pain receded enough for Seth to breathe, to think.

"I knew you were telling the truth," He gasped, looking into her eyes. "I'm sorry I doubted you."

"Later," she said with a ghost of her old smile. "Let's survive this first."

A roar of fury drew their attention. Sebastian had fought his way through the Rose and Raven Society members, leaving a trail of blood and bodies. His monstrous form launched toward them, claws extended for a final, desperate attack.

"The power is mine!" he shrieked. "It belongs to me!"

Faith intercepted him, ritual blade raised high. Her intention was clear in her eyes. She would drive the blade through Sebastian's heart, pinning him in place as the chamber collapsed around them. A suicide attack.

"Wait!" Seth shouted. "No more sacrifices!"

Drawing on the power still coursing through him, Seth released a focused burst of energy. The ritual blade flew from Faith's hand, driven by Seth's will, and embedded itself in Sebastian's chest. The vampire screamed as the blade pinned him to the wall. He re-directed the the same energy pulse back to knock Faith clear, sending her tumbling safely away from Sebastian's reach.

Seth returned his attention back to Sebastian who was still pinned against the wall, the vampire's monstrous form thrashing against the silver blade embedded in his chest. Blood, darker than human, almost black, oozed around the wound. The chamber continued to shake, reality fracturing around them as the interrupted ritual destabilized.

"It won't hold him for long," Faith warned, scrambling to her feet. "Silver only weakens him."

Seth nodded. "Think Seth, think." He said. He gripped the manuscript before him, the dual narrative he'd created remained a weapon, but it wasn't enough. The ritual was still incomplete, suspended in a dangerous state that threatened to tear apart the barrier between worlds.

"I need to finish it," Seth said, his voice steadier than he felt. "Complete the manuscript."

Emily gripped his arm. "How? The ritual's collapsing."

Seth met her gaze, struck by the strange beauty of her eyes. "It's not collapsing but instead transforming. The previous biographers showed me what to do."

He staggered back to the seventh desk, which had somehow remained intact despite the chaos. The quill lay where he'd dropped it, still stained with his blood. Seth picked it up, wondering if his blood had coagulated so he could no longer write with it. He tried it and it flowed. The magic must preserve it.

"Whatever you're planning, hurry!" Higgins shouted, still maintaining his containment circle as cracks spread across the chamber floor. "The eclipse is going to be on the waning side at any moment!"

Seth bent over the manuscript, dipping the quill in the blood that still flowed from the cut on his finger. The well kept it preserved too. The words came easily now, flowing from some deeper place of understanding. He wrote of Sebastian's true nature careful not to write too much about the monster he'd become, but the man he once was.

As he wrote, Seth felt the resonance building. The dual narrative—truth and falsehood occupying the same space, created a magical frequency that vibrated through the chamber. The crystals surrounding Emily's altar began to crack, hairline fractures spreading across their surfaces.

Sebastian screamed, a sound of pure agony. The vampire's monstrous form began to shift, scales receding, wings withering. But something else was happening too. His face was changing, aging rapidly. Wrinkles appeared around his eyes, spreading across once-perfect skin. His hair, previously midnight black, streaked with gray, then white.

"What's happening to him?" Faith asked, moving to Seth's side.

"His immortality," Seth replied, never stopping his writing. "It's unraveling. The paradox in the manuscript is disrupting the magic that sustains him."

Sebastian thrashed against the wall, his voice cracking as he howled. "Stop! You don't understand what you're doing!"

Seth continued writing, each word accelerating Sebastian's aging. Centuries of preserved youth caught up in moments. His skin began sagging, muscles atrophying, bones becoming brittle. The vampire who had terrorized them looked increasingly human, increasingly frail.

Emily approached Sebastian cautiously, her expression conflicted. "I can feel it," she whispered. "The connection between us. His blood in my veins."

Seth paused, looking up from the manuscript. "Emily?"

"I have a choice," she said, her voice distant. "I can feel it. The vampire nature he forced on me... I can embrace it. Channel it. Maybe even save him."

Sebastian's eyes, now rheumy with age, fixed on Emily. "Yes," he rasped. "You understand. You can still complete the transformation. Become what you were meant to be."

Seth trembled. Was Emily having doubts? "Or you can reject it," he said. "You can choose to embrace your humanity instead."

Emily looked between them, caught between worlds in more ways than one. The eclipse continued overhead, the moon slowly beginning to emerge from Earth's shadow. Time was running out.

"The eclipse ends soon," Higgins warned. "Whatever decision you make, it must be now."

Sebastian's aged face contorted with desperation. "Listen to me," he pleaded, his voice barely audible. "I was like you once, Seth. A biographer chosen to chronicle Mortus. I was manipulated, transformed, bound to his purpose."

Seth approached cautiously, manuscript in hand. "What are you saying?"

"My centuries of feeding, of predation, it wasn't just for survival." Sebastian's withered hand clutched at the silver blade still embedded in his chest. "It was service. Preparation. Mortus required seven biographers, seven vessels of creative energy."

"You were the first," Seth realized. "Mortus' first biographer."

Sebastian nodded, his head barely able to support the movement. "And I won't be the last. Mortus has other servants. They will continue his work when I'm gone."

Emily stepped closer to Sebastian, her form flickering between states more rapidly now. The eclipse was ending, forcing her to choose. "Is that supposed to make me sympathetic? After what you've done to me? To Seth?"

"Not sympathy," Sebastian whispered. "Understanding. The choice you have before you now. I faced it too, centuries ago. I chose wrong."

Seth looked Emily directly in her eyes, "That's the third origin story I have heard from him."

"No, this one is the truth." Sabastian rasped.

"I have made my choice," she said as the moon left the eclipse. I choose my human side."

Sabastian fell to ashes as soon as the moon cleared the eclipse.

Chapter 22
Broken Dreams of Immortality

Seth staggered through the crumbling corridor, one arm supporting Emily while the other clutched Faith's shoulder. The castle shuddered around them, ancient stones groaning as the magical backlash tore through its foundations. Behind them, Higgins and Beth struggled with Connie's limp body between them, her blood leaving a trail across the dusty floor.

"The tunnel entrance is just ahead!" Faith shouted over the din of collapsing masonry. "Move!"

Seth's lungs burned with each breath. The ritual's power still coursed through his veins, making his vision swim between this world and glimpses of the threshold realm. He could see shadowy figures retreating through cracks in reality. He could also see the lesser vampires fleeing the destruction of their master's domain.

"Connie's fading," Higgins called, his voice strained. "We need to hurry!"

Seth glanced back. Connie's face was ashen, blood soaking through her jacket where a jagged piece of ceiling had pierced her shoulder. She'd thrown herself between Higgins and a cascade of falling stone, saving the older man but taking the brunt of the impact.

"Almost there," Seth gasped, pulling Emily forward as another tremor shook the passage.

The tunnel entrance appeared ahead, a narrow archway leading to darkness. Faith reached it first, she ushered them through. Seth helped Emily across the threshold, then turned back for the others.

A deafening crack split the air as the ceiling began to give way. Higgins and Beth lunged forward with Connie between them, barely clearing the archway as tons of stone crashed down behind them, sealing the passage forever.

"Run!" Faith shouted, already moving deeper into the tunnel. "The whole system could collapse!"

Seth stumbled forward, his enhanced senses picking up the subtle shifts in the earth around them. The tunnel groaned under the strain of the castle's destruction above. He could feel the exact moment when the ritual chamber imploded, a psychic shockwave that nearly drove him to his knees.

"Am I ever going to be free of this connection to the ritual? Seth asked. "I need to get rid of this residual energy."

"Yes, it should dissipate soon. Higgins responded.

They pressed on through the darkness, Faith leading with a small flashlight, Higgins and Beth struggling to carry Connie.

The tunnel seemed endless, twisting through the cliff's interior like a stone serpent. Seth guided them through it toward safety.

"Left here," he called out, surprising himself. "There's a cave opening ahead."

Faith shot him a questioning look but followed his direction. Sure enough, the tunnel widened into a natural cavern, its far end opening onto the cliffside overlooking the sea.

They emerged into the cool night air just as the last of the castle disappeared into the earth with a thunderous roar. From their vantage point on the cliff, they watched as centuries of evil crumbled into dust, burying Sebastian's powdered remains beneath an avalanche of ancient stone.

Seth helped lower Connie to the ground as Higgins tore open a medical kit. "How bad?" he asked.

"She'll live," Higgins replied, as he prepared a syringe of pain reliever. "If we get her proper care soon."

Emily stood at the cliff's edge, her silhouette stark against the night sky. Seth joined her, watching as the last of the castle's towers disappeared into a cloud of dust and debris.

"How do you feel?" he asked softly.

"Different," she replied, turning to face him. Her eyes still carried that strange dual quality, a kind of human warmth overlaid with something otherworldly. "I can feel both sides of myself now. The human and... the other."

"Do you regret your choice?"

Emily shook her head. "No. By choosing my humanity while accepting what he made me become, I've found balance." She flexed her fingers, watching as they briefly became translucent before solidifying again. "I'll never be truly human again, but

I won't have to live under the restrictions of being a vampire either."

Seth chuckled.

Emily smiled too, "What?"

"I was just thinking. In a way, you have achieved what Sabastian was after. Immortality and vampirism without the restrictions."

"It's not quite the same, but I understand what you mean."

He felt the manuscript in his pocket grow warm, then hot. Pulling it out, he watched as the pages began to smoke, then burst into flame. The fire didn't burn his skin, consuming only the parchment until nothing remained but ash that scattered on the sea breeze. "Darn it, I grabbed that thing and carried it all the way out. I wanted that manuscript."

"Its purpose is fulfilled," Higgins said, appearing beside them. "But the power you absorbed, Seth...that remains."

Seth looked down at his hands. They appeared normal, but he could see energy flowing beneath his skin, a subtle luminescence visible only to his altered perception. "Oh Yeah. I'm not sure I like that. What's happening to me?"

"If my theory is correct, you've become something the Rose and Raven Society has never encountered before," Higgins said, his voice laden with wonder and maybe a little concern too. "A true Chronicler, whose written words can reshape reality itself."

"How is that possible?" Seth asked. "I'm not sure about that at all. What's your theory based on?"

"Well, if you're going to make me say it again. Words are merely comprised of symbols you have trained your brain to understand," Higgins explained.

Seth nodded, "I know, I know, symbols hold power."

"That's right, but what you may be unaware of is that it's symbols that lock the gates of hell and keep evil at bay and protect churches. Basically, it's symbols that bind everything in this world. A chronicler can use symbols to achieve just about any goal. I think you should officially join the Rose and Raven Society so together we can explore and train your abilities. I am afraid if you go off on your own without us, you will be dead in months from blood loss or worse."

"So, how do you know how to train me. Will my abilities keep growing?"

Faith joined them, catching the tail end of what he was saying." He has abilities now, huh. So what does that make him? Human? Something else?"

"Both," Emily answered before Higgins could respond. "Like me."

Seth watched as Higgins finished bandaging Connie's shoulder. The older man's hands moved with practiced efficiency, suggesting this wasn't the first field injury he'd treated. Probably not even the hundredth, Seth realized. How many supernatural encounters had Higgins survived over the decades?

"That should hold until we reach proper medical care," Higgins said, securing the last bandage. He straightened up with a groan, his knees cracking as he stood. "We need to move soon. Dawn's approaching."

Faith and Higgins helped Connie to a sitting position on a nearby boulder. Faith offered her water from her canteen. The two women had formed an unexpected bond during their escape from the castle. Seth noticed how Faith's usual guardedness had softened around Connie.

Higgins observed them for a moment, then cleared his throat. "Faith, I've been meaning to ask you something."

She looked up, wariness returning to her expression. "What?"

"The White Covenant clearly doesn't appreciate your talents," Higgins said. "Your combat skills, your strategic thinking, your loyalty to those who deserve it are all qualities the Rose and Raven Society values highly."

Faith's eyebrows rose. "Are you offering me a job?"

"I'm offering you a place," Higgins corrected. "A permanent position with the Society. We could use someone with your particular set of skills."

Nearby, Seth watched Faith's face, trying to read her reaction. Her expression remained carefully neutral, but he caught the flicker of interest in her eyes.

"What about my history with the White Covenant?" she asked. "They don't take kindly to deserters."

"The Society has protected its own for centuries," Higgins replied. "And frankly, after tonight's events, I suspect the White Covenant will have more pressing concerns than tracking down a single former member."

Faith glanced at Seth, then at Emily, who stood a few feet away waiting for her reply. "I'll think about it," she said finally.

Seth stepped closer to Higgins. "About exploring my abilities and training me." He flexed his fingers, "What exactly am I supposed to do with this power? Chronicle vampire rituals for the rest of my life?"

Higgins chuckled. "Sebastian was merely one threat among many, Seth. The world is full of phenomena that require investigation, documentation, and occasionally intervention."

"Like what?" Seth asked, curiosity piqued despite his exhaustion. "What else is out there?"

Higgins gazed out at the horizon, where the first hints of dawn were beginning to lighten the sky. "Where to begin? There are entities that predate human civilization like ancient gods sleeping beneath the earth or in the depths of the oceans. There are creatures that slip between dimensions, appearing only under specific circumstances."

"You're talking about cryptids? Monsters?" Seth pressed.

"Some, yes." Higgins noted. "The Rose and Raven Society has documented thousands over the centuries. Shapeshifters in the forests of Eastern Europe. Psychic parasites that feed on dreams. Entities that can manipulate time and space."

Emily drifted closer, drawn by the conversation. "You're serious, aren't you?"

"Entirely." Higgins turned to face them fully. "Take Spring-heeled Jack, for instance. In the 1830s, London was terrorized by reports of a figure who could leap impossible heights, breathe blue flames, and had glowing red eyes."

"I've heard of that," Seth said. "Victorian urban legend, right?"

"Not quite." Higgins smiled grimly. "Alastair Ravenscroft and Thaddeus Rose, the Society's founders, investigated the case personally. What they discovered was neither human nor entirely supernatural, but something in between. A being that fed on fear who could manipulate its own physical form."

Seth felt a chill, "Did they stop it?"

"They contained it," Higgins replied. "Or so they believed. Reports of similar entities have surfaced periodically since then, suggesting either their solution was temporary or there are more such creatures in existence."

"And you want us to help you hunt these things?" Faith asked, her voice skeptical but intrigued.

"I want the best and brightest minds to investigate them," Higgins corrected. "To understand them. Knowledge is our primary weapon, though sometimes more direct intervention becomes necessary."

Seth exchanged glances with Emily. Her eyes held the same mix of trepidation and fascination he felt. After everything they'd experienced with Sebastian, the idea that there were other supernatural threats in the world should have terrified him. Instead, he felt a strange sense of purpose stirring.

"What else?" Seth asked. "What other creatures has the Society encountered?"

"I'll tell you what. Let's find Connie medical attention and wrap up the case. We have a few loose ends to tie up. Once we get back to the cottage, we can sit and have tea over a lengthy conversation.

"Yes, of course," Seth said. "I didn't mean to ignore Connie's injuries. Here, I'll help you get her to the town doctor."

Chapter 23
Confined to Shadow

Seth stood at the window of the Rose and Raven Society's main conference room, watching London's evening traffic crawl through the streets below. One month since Cornwall. One month since Sebastian's castle had collapsed into the sea. The physical wounds had mostly healed, but the other challenges were still unfolding.

Behind him, voices rose and fell as the Society's senior members debated his future. Their future. He stared at the leather-bound journal Higgins had given him. He said it had specially treated paper designed to absorb the energy of his words without manifesting them physically. He said Seth's abilities were strong enough to manifest such creatures out of thin air and he would just as soon keep them hidden away...far away.

"The Vancouver nest has gone completely silent," Nigel reported, tapping a red pin on the world map spread across the conference table. "And our contacts in Prague report unusual movement among Sebastian's former allies there."

"They're consolidating," Higgins said, his voice grave. "Sebastian's death has created a power vacuum just as we feared."

Seth turned from the window. Faith sat near the head of the table, looking surprisingly comfortable in the Society's formal attire. Her official induction ceremony had been yesterday. It was a solemn affair with ancient oaths and rituals that seemed to satisfy something in her that the White Covenant never had.

Connie entered the room, leaning heavily on a silver-headed cane. Her recovery had been remarkable given the severity of her injuries, but Higgins had confirmed she would likely walk with a limp for the rest of her life. She caught Seth watching and offered a wink.

"Don't look so gloomy," she said, settling into the chair beside him. "Some of us wear our battle scars proudly."

"Some scars are more visible than others," Seth replied, tapping his temple.

Emily slipped into the room last, her movements carrying that strange fluid grace she'd developed since Cornwall. She was human enough to walk in daylight, but also vampire enough to sense the otherworldly. The perfect bridge between worlds. She was too valuable an asset to let go. Higgins had to recruit her. Being able to sense the unknown was a useful thing. He should know. He could do it as well.

"Sorry I'm late," she said, taking the empty seat on Seth's other side. "I was reviewing the Prague reports."

"And?" Higgins prompted.

"They're definitely searching for something." Emily pushed a folder across the table. "Artifacts from Sebastian's private collection have surfaced on the black market. Others have simply vanished."

"They're looking for another vessel," Seth said, the realization hitting him suddenly. "For Mortus."

The room fell silent. Higgins nodded slowly. "That's our assessment as well. Sebastian may be gone, but his master's servants remain. The ritual failed, but the knowledge of how to perform it still exists."

Seth's hand tightened around his new journal. Three days ago, he'd written a passage describing a storm, and lightning had shattered the windows of his apartment. Last week, a character sketch had manifested as a shadow figure that lingered for hours before dissipating. His words carried power now, but they were unpredictable. Until he got a handle on it, it was a dangerous power.

"Which brings us to the matter at hand," Beth said, her silver hair gleaming in the lamplight. "Seth's position within the Society."

"He should be under constant supervision," Nigel argued. "His abilities are unprecedented and unstable."

"He's not a prisoner," Emily countered, her voice sharp. "Or a weapon to be aimed and fired."

"No one is suggesting—" Higgins began.

"Aren't you?" Emily interrupted. "I've read the protocols for 'exceptional assets.' Controlled housing, monitored communications, prescribed missions."

Seth felt a chill. He'd suspected something similar, but hearing it confirmed made his stomach twist. "Sounds a lot like what Sebastian offered. Protection in exchange for service."

"This is completely different," Beth insisted. "The Society exists to understand and contain supernatural threats."

"And what am I?" Seth asked quietly. "A threat or an asset?"

The question hung in the air. Faith broke the silence with a short laugh. "Both, obviously. Just like the rest of us."

"The point," Emily continued, "is that binding Seth to the Society's protocols would repeat the same patterns of control that Sebastian established. Different intentions, perhaps, but the same fundamental dynamic."

Seth watched Higgins' face as he absorbed Emily's words. The older man had been nothing but supportive, but Seth had seen the fascination in his eyes when witnessing Seth's abilities manifest. The scholar's hunger for knowledge wasn't so different from Sebastian's hunger for power.

"What do you propose instead?" Higgins asked finally.

"Partnership," Emily said simply. "Seth and I work with the Society, not for it. We investigate cases that require our unique abilities but maintain our independence."

"That's unprecedented," Nigel protested.

"So is everything about this situation," Connie pointed out, tapping her cane for emphasis. "Maybe unprecedented problems require unprecedented solutions."

Seth met Emily's gaze across the table, feeling the unique connection they'd forged in Cornwall. She understood what he was going through better than anyone. She knew the disorientation of becoming something other than human, the struggle to maintain identity when reality itself seemed malleable.

"I need to learn control," Seth admitted. "But I won't become anyone's tool again."

"Why don't the three of you work together? Faith has a lot to offer." Higgins suggested.

Seth coughed, "Have you forgotten I left Faith for Emily. I have dated them both."

"And now you date neither." Higgins countered.

"We are all adults, Seth." Emily said.

"Yes, we are." Faith added. "I am over it. I have no problems working with you and Emily. I look at it all with a new perspective. None of us is even remotely the same as we were when this all started."

"Well, if you think I need two babysitters to control myself and not hemorrhage myself to death, who am I to argue with the great leader of the Rose and Raven Society."

"You will all have to go through the standard training before I can allow you back into the field. I know you feel like you have already been in the field, and you have done fine but I will take no arguments. You must know how we operate, where the safe houses are, and where the underground resources are located. You have to know the secret code language we use and so on. I will issue you all the official handbook."

"We have a handbook?" Seth asked, a hint of sarcasm in his voice.

"Of course we do." Beth answered, "And you are going to study it!"

"Yes, ma'am." Seth said.

Seth hunched over his desk, the plastic keys of the keyboard clacking loudly as he completed another chapter of Sebastian's true biography. Not the poisoned manuscript that had disrupted the ritual, but an accurate, clinical account of the vampire's existence. The words flowed easily now that he'd learned to control some of his abilities, though he still kept a box of tissues nearby for the occasional nosebleed. He wasn't sure if he would publish the unauthorized biography or if it would just be filed away in the Rose and Raven archives.

"You've been at it for six hours straight," Emily said, placing a cup of coffee beside him. "Even chroniclers need breaks."

Seth rubbed his eyes, leaning back in his chair. "Almost done with the Victorian era section. Did you know Sebastian might have been responsible for at least three of the murders attributed to Jack the Ripper?"

"Not surprising." Emily perched on the edge of his desk, "you have proof?" She'd gained remarkable control over her dual nature in the months since Cornwall. "Come to think of it, he always did have a flair for the theatrical."

"I said may be responsible so no, I have no proof. It does make the story interesting if it's true though." He paused, "Don't worry, I didn't write it as a falsehood. I just presented the evidence. If they put this biography in the archives, I want it to be as accurate as possible."

Seth saved his work, careful to use the specially designed computer Higgins had provided. One isolated from networks and shielded against magical interference. His words carried too much power now to risk them spreading uncontrolled.

"It's likely they will. The Society's archivists are already building the vampire catalog based on your earlier chapters," Emily continued. "They're cross-referencing with historical accounts, identifying bloodlines and weaknesses."

"And that's why I'm being careful about what I include," Seth said, tapping the screen. "Nothing about vampires like Sebastian, the ones who feed on creativity and emotion. No details about their rituals or powers. I wouldn't want them to feed off my work."

"Smart. We don't want to inadvertently strengthen them through documentation."

Seth chuckled, "Like they would ever get to read it, but I guess you can never be too careful. I do try to remember Higgins' warning: some knowledge is too dangerous to preserve, even in the Society's secure archives. Words have power etcetera.

"Do me a favor. I am a big girl, but Sabastian did traumatize me a bit. I would rather we moved passed him and not dignify him by remembering him too often after you finish the biography of course."

"You got it. I kind of want to leave him in the past as well. What else you got?"

"Well, I guess more on Sabastian."

"Ironic considering we just agreed to stop talking about him."

"I said after you finish the biography. We can discuss him up until then."

"All right, what is the news?"

"Faith called while you were writing," her tone carefully neutral. "The team in Prague found something."

Seth's attention sharpened. Faith had been leading a Society expedition to investigate sites connected to Sebastian's past. "What did they find?"

"Magical residue at the castle ruins. Similar to Cornwall, but older. Much older." Emily handed him her tablet, displaying images of glowing symbols etched into ancient stone. "The patterns match Sebastian's ritual chamber, but carbon dating puts these at least two thousand years old."

"That lying bastard," Seth muttered, examining the images. "He claimed he was turned during World War II, then I read in his journal it was the 1700s. But these..."

"Suggest he was ancient," Emily finished. "Possibly Roman era or earlier."

Seth felt a chill. Sebastian had been playing a much longer game than any of them had realized. "Does Higgins know?"

"He's assembling an emergency council meeting. Faith's team found something else." Emily's expression turning grave. "Evidence of at least three other ritual sites across Europe and Asia. All with the same basic configuration, seven writing stations arranged around a central altar."

"Other vampires attempting the same ritual?" Seth's stomach dropped.

"That's the working theory. Sebastian wasn't unique and he was probably part of a pattern. Ancient vampires all seeking the same goal: ascension beyond their limitations."

Seth closed his eyes, remembering Sebastian's final words: "Mortus has other servants. They will continue his work when I'm gone." Not a desperate lie, but a warning.

"The council believes we've stumbled into something bigger than Sebastian," Emily continued. "A coordinated effort spanning centuries, maybe millennia. These elder vampires have been patient, methodical. They have each cultivating their seven biographers across generations."

Seth thought of the preserved bodies in the crypt beneath Cornwall Castle. Six previous writers, their creative essence harvested to fuel Sebastian's ritual. How many other crypts existed around the world? How many other writers had been manipulated, drained, and discarded?

"We need to identify them," Seth said. "All of them, the vampires and their potential biographers."

"That's why your biography is so important," Emily replied. "It's becoming the foundation for understanding how these rituals work, how to recognize the patterns before they're complete."

Seth turned back to his computer, a new urgency driving him. "I'll finish the Victorian section tonight and start on the twentieth century tomorrow. The more we understand about Sebastian's methods, the better chance we have of stopping the others."

"Just don't push yourself too hard," Emily cautioned, her hand cool against his shoulder. "We defeated one ancient vampire. We'll find a way to stop the others too."

Seth agreed. Sebastian had been just one piece in a larger puzzle, and that puzzle was full of dimensions they were only beginning to comprehend. The war had barely begun.

Chapter 24
The Path of the Chronicler

Seth stood peering out the window of his and Emily's Scottish safehouse, watching the rain fall against ancient stone. The highlands stretched before him, misty and primeval, the perfect backdrop for what had become his daily routine. Three months since Cornwall, and he still struggled to control the power that flowed through his veins.

"Focus," he muttered to himself, opening his leather-bound journal. The specially treated pages could absorb the energy of his words without manifesting them physically...most of the time. He'd learned that lesson the hard way after describing a thunderstorm and nearly burning down their cottage. He was practicing every day, but he didn't have it down perfect quite yet. The words did have power but not every word used the power within him to manifest things. It was mostly for scribing symbols of protection or to keep nasty things trapped or at bay. Only things in the natural world could be manifested anyway. Wind, rain, light, lightning and that sort of thing could be produced with his words, but something like a car or a mug of coffee could not be conjured simply by writing down the words.

Seth wrote carefully, describing a simple red apple. A single piece of fruit counted as something from the natural world, and he had not had a fresh apple in a while. He concentrated on channeling the energy through his fingertips, visualizing the fruit in perfect detail while containing the manifestation to a small area on the desk before him. The air shimmered, molecules rearranging themselves according to his written command.

A red apple materialized, hovering an inch above the wooden surface. Perfect in shape, color, and Seth plucked it from the air, substance. He took a bite. Sweet, crisp, real.

"Getting better," Emily said from the doorway. She moved with that fluid grace that still caught him off guard sometimes.

"Still can't manage anything more complex without a nosebleed," Seth admitted, tossing her the apple.

Emily caught it one-handed and took a bite. "Progress is progress. Three weeks ago, you tried to manifest a cup of coffee and flooded the kitchen with beans."

Seth winced at the memory. "That's before I figured out how writing the words work. The beans were the natural part. The beans ground and processed into coffee is not a natural state. How was your hunt?"

"Productive." Emily wiped a faint trace of blood from her lips. She'd been out since dawn, tracking deer through the highlands. Her unique condition required blood occasionally, but she'd refused to feed on humans. "The transformation is stabilizing. I can go longer between feedings now."

Seth nodded, relieved. Emily's dual nature had been volatile at first, swinging between human vulnerability and vampiric hunger. He had offered himself, but she would not hear of it. Now she maintained an equilibrium that gave her unprecedented insight into vampire psychology without sacrificing her humanity.

"Any word from Faith?" he asked, closing his journal.

"Nothing new. You saw the last report. As far as I know her team is still tracking ritual sites in Prague." Emily settled into the chair opposite him. "The Society's keeping her busy."

Seth tried not to worry. Faith had been training as a field agent since the time of their romantic breakup, and her leadership of the Prague expedition made sense. Still, he couldn't shake the feeling that something was wrong. The Society's communications had grown increasingly cryptic over the past few weeks.

A knock at the door interrupted his thoughts. Emily tensed, moving to the window with preternatural speed.

"Delivery van," she reported. "Single driver."

Seth approached the door cautiously. Living off the grid meant packages were rare and usually arranged through Higgins. He opened the door to find a courier holding a small, unmarked box.

"Delivery for Aubrey," the man said, his Scottish accent thick.

Seth signed for the package and brought it inside, turning it over in his hands. No return address, no markings of any kind. "Scan it?"

Emily nodded, placing her hands on the box and closing her eyes. Her ability to sense magical energies had grown stronger with practice. "No traps, no wards. Just... paper inside. And something metal."

Seth cut the tape carefully. Inside lay a jumble of torn paper fragments and a small silver compass. He spread the pieces across the table, recognizing Faith's handwriting immediately.

"It's from Faith," he said, arranging the fragments. "Looks like she tore up her notes and sent them to us."

Emily leaned over his shoulder. "Why not just call?"

"Maybe she couldn't." Seth pieced together the first fragment: *...discovered third ritual site. Configuration matches Cornwall exactly. Carbon dating confirms...*

Another piece: *...Higgins isn't responding to my reports. Something's wrong with Society communications...*

And another: *...team disappeared last night. Only Janssen and I remain. We're being watched...*

Seth's stomach tightened as he assembled more fragments: *...not what we thought. Sebastian wasn't working alone. There's a network...*

The final piece contained coordinates scrawled in hasty numbers and a message that made Seth's blood run cold: *The Eldest wakes. Come ASAP.*

"Eastern Europe," Emily said, examining the coordinates. She plugged them into her GPS device. "These coordinates are near the Carpathian Mountains."

"Of course they are. The Carpathians are vampire central." Seth picked up the silver compass. It wasn't ordinary—the needle pointed not north, but toward the coordinates Faith had provided. "She's in trouble."

"Or it's a trap," Emily countered. "Why send a package instead of using Society channels?"

"Because she doesn't trust them anymore." Seth gathered the fragments. "Look at what she wrote here. Higgins isn't responding, her team disappeared. Something's wrong with the Society. We had better try to see if we can contact them ourselves."

Emily paced the room, "Two mysteries in opposite directions. If Faith's right and Sebastian was part of a network, the Society could be compromised. Remember Davies?"

Seth nodded grimly. "He did claim there were others like him, infiltrators serving vampire masters. I had assumed the measures Higgins took when he got back to headquarters took care of that."

"I assumed as well."

"We need to go to these coordinates," Seth said, pocketing the compass. "Faith wouldn't have reached out unless it was serious."

"You think we should split up? You go to Faith, and I go to Rose and Raven."

"Not on your life. We will try to contact the Society and if we can't, we will check on them after we go help Faith. I am not splitting up after everything we've been through. If anything, I am going to make sure we all three come together."

"All right." She picked up one of the torn fragments, "The Eldest wakes," Emily repeated. "If she means Mortus..."

"Or something worse." Seth opened his laptop, already searching for the fastest route to Eastern Europe. "Pack what you need. We leave tonight."

"I will get our luggage from the closet."

Seth began the task of figuring out the secrets of the silver compass in his palm, its needle unwavering in its eastward direction. He glanced again at the torn fragments of Faith's message that lay scattered across the table like pieces of a puzzle he couldn't quite solve. Something about "The Eldest wakes" sent a chill down his spine that had nothing to do with the Scottish highland winds howling outside their safehouse.

A sharp knock at the door made him jump. Emily moved from the bedroom to the window in one fluid motion, almost too fast for Seth to follow her movement.

"It's Higgins," she said, surprise in her voice. "And he's not alone."

Seth tucked the compass into his pocket and opened the door. Higgins stood on the threshold, his tweed jacket damp from the misty rain, his expression grim. Behind him, Connie leaned on her silver-headed cane, her face drawn with exhaustion.

"This is unexpected," Seth said, stepping aside to let them enter. "I was just about to use the satellite phone to call you."

"What brings you all the way out here?" Emily asked.

"Necessity, not courtesy, I'm afraid," Higgins replied, removing his rain-spattered glasses. "We have a situation."

Emily brought towels and made tea while Higgins spread a series of photographs across the table, covering Faith's torn notes. Each image showed something impossible. The first image was of a werewolf caught in mid-transformation on a London street camera; next was a ghoul feeding in a Paris cemetery; another had a vampire attack in broad daylight in Tokyo.

"These were all taken within the last seventy-two hours," Higgins said, tapping the photos. "There's been an unprecedented surge in supernatural activity worldwide. All manner of creatures including vampires, ghouls, ghosts, and werepeople all manifesting with increasing frequency and decreasing subtlety. There is so much going on the members of the Rose and Raven Society are spread far too thin."

Seth picked up the Tokyo photograph. "They're not even trying to hide anymore."

"That's what's most concerning," Connie added, settling into a chair with a wince. Her injury from Cornwall still pained her. "Something is causing the realm of the unknown to become more prominent again. The veil between worlds is thinning."

"What about Faith?" Emily asked, placing mugs of tea before them. "We just received a package from her, and you just placed the photographs over her torn messages. She claims her team has disappeared and you weren't responding to her reports."

Higgins sighed heavily. "That's the other reason we're here. There's been a communication breakdown at Society headquarters. No one's been manning the phones."

"No one's been—" Seth began incredulously.

"I've been trying to hire someone," Higgins cut in defensively, "but the process is lengthy given the secrecy and sensitive nature of the Society. Background checks, magical aptitude tests, loyalty spells, it's not like posting an ad on LinkedIn."

Seth exchanged glances with Emily. "We were just about to head to these coordinates." He pulled out the silver compass and Faith's note with the location. "Faith seems to think something big is happening there."

Higgins studied the coordinates, his expression darkening. "The Carpathians. Of course."

"We need to find her," Seth insisted. "If what she wrote is true—if the Eldest is waking—"

"I agree," Higgins said, surprising him. "You and Emily should go immediately. Your unique abilities make you particularly suited for this mission. You can track and protect people before vampires and other creatures can exploit them."

Seth hadn't expected Higgins to acquiesce so readily. "You're letting us go into the field? Just like that?"

"The situation is dire enough to warrant exceptional measures," Higgins replied. "Besides, Connie and I were already on our way to investigate another matter in Great Britain. The timing is... convenient."

Connie tapped her cane against the floor. "I can fill you in on Society resources in the Carpathian Mountains. We maintain several safe houses and have contacts in most major cities. You'll need them."

As Connie outlined the network of Society allies and safe houses throughout Eastern Europe, Seth felt a strange pressure building behind his eyes. The room around him began to blur, sounds becoming distant and muffled. He gripped the edge of the table, trying to steady himself.

"Seth?" Emily's voice seemed to come from very far away.

Higgins grabbed Emily's hand before she went to him. "I don't think he's done this since Cornwall, since he was connected to you in fact. He's having a vision. If you want to help him, get something for the blood that's about to flow."

"He's been practicing." Emily said. I doubt he will bleed...much."

Seth heard Higgins and Emily talking but he couldn't respond. The safehouse abruptly disappeared. Instead, Seth found himself standing in an ancient library, its vaulted ceilings lost in shadow. Towering shelves stretched in every direction, filled with manuscripts bound in leather similar to Sebastian's journal. In the center of the room stood Faith, her face gaunt with exhaustion, her clothes torn and dirty. She looked directly at him, her eyes wide with recognition as if she were surprised he had actually appeared.

She mouthed something—no sound reached him, but he could read her lips clearly: "Find the first book."

Faith reached toward him, desperation in her eyes, but before their hands could meet, the vision shattered. Seth gasped, finding himself back in the safehouse, Emily's concerned face inches from his own.

"What happened?" she demanded. "Higgin's says you had a vision."

"I did. I saw her," Seth managed, his voice hoarse. "Faith. She was in some kind of ancient library filled with manuscripts. They were all old like Sebastian's journal. She told me to 'find the first book.'"

Higgins leaned forward, suddenly intent. "Did you see anything else? Any identifying features of the library?"

Seth shook his head, the afterimage of those endless shelves still burning in his mind. "Just books. Hundreds, maybe thousands of them. And Faith, looking like she hadn't slept in days."

"Your abilities are evolving," Connie observed. "This wasn't just a vision—it was contact across distance."

"And no blood!" Higgins said, "Bravo!"

"We need to leave now," Emily said, already moving to gather their luggage and equipment. "If Faith is still alive, she won't be for long."

Chapter 25
The First Book

Seth and Emily trudged through fresh snow as they approached the crumbling stone structure nestled against the mountainside. The silver compass in his palm vibrated slightly, its needle pointing directly at the ancient monastery that loomed before them. After three days of grueling travel through the Carpathian wilderness, they had finally reached Faith's coordinates.

"This can't be right," Seth muttered, squinting at the decrepit building. "It looks like it's been abandoned for centuries."

Emily moved ahead, her heightened senses scanning the area. "Appearances can be deceiving. I smell... paper. Old paper and ink. Lots of it."

The monastery's facade was weathered by time, its stone walls partially reclaimed by nature. No lights shone from within, no smoke rose from chimneys. Yet as they drew closer, Seth felt a familiar pressure building behind his eyes—the same sensation he'd experienced during his vision of Faith.

"She's here," he said with certainty. "Or was recently."

They approached the heavy wooden doors, their ancient hinges groaning in protest as Emily pushed them open. The interior was surprisingly intact, but it was dusty and cold. It was also enclosed and protected from the elements. Faded frescoes depicting biblical scenes covered the walls, their colors muted by centuries of candle smoke.

"Look at this," Emily whispered, pointing to a symbol carved into the stone archway above them.

"It's a rose intertwined with a raven." Seth said.

"But how. It looks old, really old."

Seth traced the carving with his fingertips. "The Society's emblem. I don't understand it either. This place predates Higgins' records by centuries."

They moved deeper into the monastery, following narrow corridors lit only by the beams of their flashlights. The silver compass led them downward, past empty cells and prayer rooms, until they reached a heavy iron door set into the rock itself.

"No lock," Emily observed, running her hands over the smooth metal surface. "How do we—"

Seth placed his palm against the door, feeling the familiar tingle of energy beneath his skin. Words formed in his mind unbidden, ancient phrases in a language he shouldn't understand but somehow did. He spoke them out loud, his voice echoing strangely in the confined space.

The door swung inward silently, revealing a vast chamber beyond.

"My God," Seth breathed, stepping through the doorway.

Before them stretched an immense underground library, exactly as he had seen in his vision. Towering shelves filled with leather-bound manuscripts extended in every direction, disappearing into shadows beyond their flashlight beams. The air smelled of ancient parchment and something else. It smelled like a faint metallic tang that reminded Seth uncomfortably of blood.

"The Repository of Chroniclers," Emily read from an inscription carved in a language that even he didn't understand above an inner archway. "Established 1142."

"You can read that?" he asked.

"Yeah, I just did. You couldn't read it?"

"Nope."

"Surprising."

Seth moved toward the center of the chamber, where a large circular table stood surrounded by seven ornate chairs. The arrangement struck a disturbing chord of familiarity—too similar to Sebastian's ritual chamber for comfort.

"This predates the Rose and Raven Society," Seth said, examining the ancient texts on the table. "This is where it all began."

"Seth!" Emily's voice echoed from several rows away. "I found something."

He followed her voice to find her standing before a glass case containing a single massive tome, its cover bound in what appeared to be human skin. The title, written in faded gold leaf, read simply: "Primus Liber"—The First Book.

"This is what Faith wanted us to find," Seth said, recognizing it instantly. "The first chronicle. I don't understand. If Faith was here, she already knew where it was, the first book."

"She might not have wanted you to discover it; she might have just wanted you to go to it. There may be something inside it she wanted you to see." Emily placed her hand on the glass, her expression troubled. "I can feel power radiating from it. Old power."

Seth carefully lifted the case, half-expecting some ancient trap to trigger, but nothing happened. The book lay before them, its pages yellowed with age but remarkably preserved. As Seth opened it, the text seemed to shift before his eyes, translating itself into modern English.

"It's responding to you," Emily observed. "To your chronicler abilities."

Seth began to read, his heart pounding with excitement and fear as the true history of vampirism unfolded before him. The book detailed how ancient mystics had discovered entities existing beyond human reality, beings of pure energy that existed outside time. These mystics had performed rituals to bind themselves to these entities, seeking immortality.

"They weren't cursed," Seth said, turning pages with growing horror. "They chose this. The first vampires deliberately bound themselves to these... things."

"And the resurrection rituals?" Emily asked.

"They're attempts to complete the binding," Seth explained, pointing to detailed diagrams in the text. "Sebastian wasn't trying to resurrect Mortus as a separate being. He was trying to fully merge with him, to transform from a mere immortal into something godlike."

Page after page revealed the truth. Vampires like Sebastian weren't isolated predators but part of an organized effort spanning millennia. Their anonymity wasn't accidental but strategic. Scholars throughout history had recognized the danger of documenting their existence, knowing that written words could either strengthen or weaken the vampires' power.

"What I can do, the way my words manifest reality, it's not unique to me," Seth realized, finding accounts of other chroniclers throughout history who had developed similar abilities after contact with vampires. "This has happened before. Many times."

"And the vampires have been hunting chroniclers all along," Emily added grimly. "Using them to fuel their transformation rituals."

"This type of vampire anyway. This page speaks of the undead variety as being a separate thing completely. These vampires have dominion over them. That's how Sabastian had the lesser vampires at his castle." Seth turned to the final pages, where a list of names stretched across the parchment. There were hundreds of them, chroniclers who had come before him. Some names were crossed out, others circled. Faith's name appeared near the bottom, recently added and underlined.

"There are more vampire elders than we ever imagined," Seth said. "And they've been operating in the shadows for centuries."

"What do you think Faith's name appears in this book? What does it mean?" Emily asked.

"I don't know. Could she have been taken as a part of this library?" A chill ran through him. "We need to find her," he whispered, about to close the book when a familiar voice echoed through the cavernous library.

"You already have."

Seth spun around, his heart leaping into his throat. He had never been so happy to see someone in his life. Faith stood between two towering bookshelves, but not the Faith he remembered. Her form shimmered at the edges. Her eyes held an otherworldly luminescence, and when she moved toward them, her feet barely seemed to touch the ground.

"Faith?" Emily stepped forward cautiously. "What happened to you?"

Faith's smile was both familiar and strange. "It was that book. I read passages from it and this happened to me. I am changed, but not like you, Emily. It did something different to me. It turns out touching that book and reading the ancient knowledge from it, if you have the ability to receive it, is transformative.

"What did you read?" Emily asked.

"I was interested in what it had to say about hunting vampires. It's written inside that those who hunt the vampires like Sabastian must complete the ritual. Once I came across the passage, I read it out loud out of habit."

Seth approached her slowly, fighting the urge to reach out and touch her, unsure if his hand would pass right through. "Are you... still human?"

"Mostly." Faith's gaze shifted to the First Book. "I see you have it. Good. We don't have much time."

"Time for what?" Seth asked.

"Sebastian's defeat created ripples. The other elders felt it. It created a disturbance in their carefully constructed order." Faith moved to the circular table, her movements fluid and unnaturally graceful. "They've accelerated their plans, sensing vulnerability in our momentary advantage."

Emily's head snapped toward the entrance. "Someone's coming. Multiple footsteps."

Faith nodded grimly. "Sebastian's former allies. They've tracked us here. More specifically, they have tracked you, even more specifically, Seth. Your abilities make you a beacon to their kind."

"How many?" Seth asked, already reaching for his journal.

"Too many," Faith replied. "A coalition of covens from across Eastern Europe, led by one of Sebastian's oldest allies. They want the book, and you."

The distant sound of footsteps grew louder, accompanied by hisses and snarls that echoed through the ancient stone corridors. Seth felt a familiar pressure building behind his eyes, his chronicler abilities responding to the approaching threat.

"We need to protect the repository," Emily said, her eyes shifting to their vampiric amber. "These texts contain too much knowledge to fall into their hands."

Faith nodded. "Emily and I can hold them off. Our abilities complement each other—I can see their movements across realities, and she has the strength to act on that knowledge."

"What about me?" Seth asked.

"The First Book," Faith said. "You need to secure it. It's too dangerous to destroy but too valuable to lose. In fact, you're probably the only one who can protect it...chronicler."

Seth nodded, understanding immediately. He turned to the ancient tome, feeling its power resonating with his own. As his fingers touched the leather binding, words formed in his mind—not just descriptions, but commands, bindings, limitations.

The first vampire minion burst through the entrance, its form more bestial than Sebastian's elegant appearance had ever been. Emily moved with blinding speed, intercepting it before it could fully enter the chamber. Faith moved with speed almost comparable to Emily. She rounded up several of the mindless fiends.

"Seth, now!" Faith called out, her voice echoing strangely as if coming from multiple locations simultaneously.

Seth opened his journal and began to write, the words flowing from his pen with newfound purpose and power. Not just descriptions of reality, but alterations to it. Bindings. Limitations. Banishments.

"By word and will, I bind thee," he wrote, feeling each syllable draw power from his essence. "Creatures of shadow, bound to flesh not your own, I limit your reach in this sacred space."

The effect was immediate and astonishing. The vampires at the entrance howled in pain and rage as invisible barriers formed around them, constraining their movements, weakening their supernatural abilities. One tried to leap across the chamber and found itself unable to cross an invisible line Seth had described in his journal.

"It's working!" Emily called out, taking advantage of her opponent's sudden weakness to drive it back.

Faith flittered between attackers, her newfound abilities allowing her to predict their movements and move to seemingly appear where she was needed most. "Keep writing, Seth! Your words are binding them!"

Seth continued, each sentence more powerful than the last as he discovered the true potential of his chronicler abilities.

"We need to go. Now. While they're contained," Faith said.

Seth nodded, carefully closing the First Book and tucking it under his arm.

"Wait, what will we do about this place. It contains centuries of knowledge, and those creatures will not stay bound forever." Seth said.

"We burn it." Faith said matter of fact.

"What, no!" Seth was horrified.

"I would have done it already, but I couldn't take the book across the threshold. I knew I need you here for that. "

"I won't let you do it." Seth said.

"Relax, all you have to do it allow the book to absorb all the other books before we burn it. Read page one thousand twenty-one." Faith told him.

"You know a lot about this book." Seth observed.

"Yeah, I spent a lot of time here waiting for you. Now hurry."

Seth read the page she told him and performed the task, following the girls out while avoiding the creatures trying to get to them. Faith tossed a can of fuel she had stowed near the entrance into the doorway and lit a match. She tossed it into the monastery. The place went up in flames even more quickly than Seth imagined.

Chapter 26
That Bastard the Vampire

Seth stumbled through the snow, clutching the First Book against his chest as if it were a shield. The heat of the burning monastery pressed against his back, flames licking skyward in a furious orange column visible for miles. Faith led the way. Emily brought up the rear, her heightened senses alert for pursuit.

"We need to get off this ridge," Faith called back, her voice carrying unnaturally through the howling mountain wind. "The rest will regroup once they realize what we've done."

Seth's lungs burned with each breath of frigid air.

"There," Emily pointed to a dark shape nestled among a stand of pines. "Some kind of structure."

"It looks like a Hunter's cabin." Faith said. "I bet it's been abandoned for years. It'll do."

The cabin materialized fully as they approached. It was a simple wooden structure with a sagging roof and boarded windows. Faith pushed open the door, which scraped on rusted hinges. Inside, dust covered every surface, but the walls were solid, and the stone fireplace remained intact.

"No one's been here in at least a decade," Emily said, scanning the single room. She moved to the fireplace, clearing cobwebs from the chimney. "But it's dry."

Seth placed the First Book on a rickety table, his arms trembling with relief as he released its weight. Blood trickled from his nose, and he wiped it away absently, too focused on their escape to worry about the physical toll of his abilities.

"Did we lose them?" he asked, collapsing onto a wooden chair that creaked dangerously beneath him.

Faith moved to the single window, peering through a gap in the boards. "For now. The fire will keep them occupied, searching for remains. They won't expect us to have saved the book."

Emily gathered kindling from a stack beside the fireplace. "We should keep the fire small. Smoke will give away our position."

"No it won't" Faith smiled. "I will mask it. I can do that now."

"Good for you." Emily said.

Seth turned his attention back to the First Book. Now that they were relatively safe, he could examine it properly. The ancient tome seemed different somehow, it felt thicker now, its pages more numerous than he remembered from the monastery.

"It's changing," he murmured, opening the cover carefully.

Faith glanced over. "The book responds to its reader. It shows what you need to see, when you need to see it."

"Convenient," Emily said.

Seth turned the pages slowly, discovering sections that hadn't been visible during his initial reading. Diagrams of ritual circles, genealogies of vampire bloodlines, accounts of previous chroniclers and their fates, information that would have taken weeks to absorb now presented itself in an order that made immediate sense to him.

"This is incredible," he whispered. "It's organizing itself for me."

Emily knelt beside him, "Wow, how is that possible?"

Seth turned another page and froze. A familiar symbol caught his eye—the same stylized 'W' that had sealed Sebastian's personal journal. The page detailed preservation rituals specific to vampires of Sebastian's lineage.

"Look at this," he said, "Vampires like Sebastian can preserve their essence through their journals if their physical form is destroyed."

Emily leaned closer. "What does that mean?"

"It means they can't truly die as long as their journals exist," Seth explained. "Their consciousness, their power—it lives on in their written words."

"Sebastian's journal," Faith said. "The one you found in his apartment."

Seth nodded grimly. "The one that burned up when the ritual collapsed. At least, I thought it did." He continued reading. The book revealed details that made his stomach twist. "According to this, the journal wouldn't have been destroyed in the fire. It would have absorbed the energy of the failed ritual, becoming a vessel for Sebastian's essence. My God! It's the true reason why he wrote it."

"Are you saying Sebastian could still be alive?" Emily asked.

"Not alive," Seth corrected, turning another page as the book revealed more secrets. "But not gone either. His consciousness could be preserved within the journal, waiting for someone to find it, to read it, and to give him a way back."

"How is this possible? "Faith asked.

"When I destroyed Sebastian's journal during the ritual, I thought that was the end of him," Seth said, his voice barely above a whisper. "But according to this, I didn't destroy the connection at all."

Faith moved closer, "What do you mean?"

"The manuscript I wrote, the one with the dual narrative, it created a paradox." Seth turned another page, revealing text that seemed to write itself before his eyes. "Truth and falsehood occupying the same space. It didn't kill Sebastian; it trapped him between worlds."

"What was those ashes he turned into then?" Emily asked.

"It was just him phasing out of this reality and into the trap I unwittingly set."

Faith closed her eyes, her new abilities allowing her to perceive beyond normal reality. "I can sense him," she confirmed after a moment. "Like a shadow, a disembodied voice. He's there, watching, waiting."

Seth slammed the book shut, his hands trembling. "We need to get to London. The Society needs to know what we've found."

Three days later, they stood in Higgins' office at Rose and Raven Society headquarters. The First Book lay open on his desk, its pages turning by themselves as if searching for specific information.

Higgins paced the room, occasionally stopping to examine Faith with undisguised fascination. "Extraordinary," he muttered. "The book gave you all these new abilities?

"Focus, Higgins," Seth said sharply. "Sebastian isn't gone. He's trapped, but gathering strength."

"Yes, yes, of course." Higgins adjusted his glasses. "And you believe your manuscript created this... pocket dimension where he now exists?"

"The paradox in my writing disrupted the ritual," Seth explained. "Instead of completing the circuit as he intended, it created a tear in reality. He fell through, but he's finding his way back."

Seth opened his journal, the pages now filled with protective symbols he'd been developing since their escape from the Carpathians. Each symbol glowed faintly.

"These wards should help secure the building," he said. "I've been experimenting with my abilities. The symbols act as anchors, reinforcing the barriers between worlds."

Emily, who had been unusually quiet since their return, moved to the window. "It may not be enough," she said, staring at the London skyline. "Look."

They joined her at the window. In the distance, a strange aurora rippled across the night sky—green and purple tendrils dancing where no such phenomenon should exist. Below, the streets seemed unusually empty for early evening.

"It's happening everywhere," Higgins said grimly. "Reports are coming in from Society branches worldwide. Supernatural manifestations increasing exponentially. Creatures that haven't been seen in centuries suddenly appearing in populated areas."

"The veil is thinning," Faith said. "Sebastian's disruption is affecting the barriers between all worlds, not just his prison."

Seth returned to his journal, adding more complex symbols to the protective wards. As he wrote, a sudden, blinding pain shot through his skull. His pen clattered to the desk as he clutched his head, blood streaming from his nose.

"Seth!" Emily was at his side instantly. "Oh no, he's hemorrhaging again."

But Seth couldn't hear her. His vision had gone dark, replaced by images that weren't his own. Sebastian, or what remained of him, floated in a void of swirling darkness. The vampire's form was translucent, incomplete, but growing more solid with each passing moment. Around him, words floated in the emptiness—Seth's words, from the biography he'd been writing.

"Stop," Seth gasped, returning to himself. "I need to stop writing about him."

"What did you see?" Faith asked, steadying him as he swayed on his feet.

"Sebastian. He's using my words, my continued documentation of his life, as energy to reconstitute himself." Seth wiped blood from his face with a shaking hand. "Every time I write about him, I'm feeding him, making him stronger."

Higgins paled. "That's extraordinary, terrifying, but extraordinary.

"Then we use it against him," Emily said. "If Seth's writing gives Sebastian power, we turn that connection into a weapon."

Three months had passed since they'd fled London with the First Book, establishing this safehouse in the ancient city of Prague's labyrinthine streets. The ornate spires and medieval architecture made Prague the perfect hunting ground for vampires, and the perfect base for those who hunted them.

He traced a symbol on the frosted glass of the picture window looking out into the snowy city, one of dozens he'd mastered since discovering his true abilities. The mark glowed briefly before fading, reinforcing the protective barriers around their building. These wards had become second nature now, requiring barely a thought to manifest.

Behind him, maps covered the walls, red pins marking confirmed vampire sightings across Europe. Black pins indicated suspected ritual sites. Yellow pins represented Society safe houses and allies. The pattern was becoming clearer with each passing week. The elder vampires were organizing, communicating, preparing for something.

Seth rubbed his temples, fighting the familiar pressure building behind his eyes. The headaches came less frequently now but still served as reminders of the price his abilities extracted. At least the nosebleeds had mostly stopped.

"Any change?" Faith called from the kitchen, where she was reviewing reports from Society field agents.

"Nothing yet," Seth replied, eyes scanning the street below. "But something feels different tonight."

The First Book lay open on the table, surrounded by Seth's notes and translations. They'd been studying it methodically, searching for weaknesses in vampire lore, particularly those like Sebastian who fed on creative energy. The traditional undead vampires were easier to track and eliminate. They could be dispatched with stakes, sunlight, and decapitation. But the psychic vampires, the emotion-feeders, the ancient ones who had willingly bound themselves to otherworldly entities required more complex solutions.

Faith emerged from the kitchen. "Higgins sent word. The Society's recruitment efforts are showing results. Twenty-seven new field agents deployed across Europe this week alone."

"Good," Seth said without turning from the window. "We need all the help we can get."

The Society had transformed in the months since Cornwall, expanding operations, modernizing methods, preparing for a war most humans didn't even know was happening. The supernatural incursions had slowed somewhat, thanks to their efforts, but Seth knew it was only the beginning.

Emily entered the room carrying a steaming mug. "You've been standing there for hours," she said, handing him the tea. "Take a break."

Seth accepted the mug gratefully, letting the warmth seep into his cold fingers. "I've been thinking about what we found in Berlin last week."

"The ritual circle?" Emily asked, moving beside him to look out at the snow-covered street.

"Seven writing desks, just like Sebastian's," Seth confirmed. "But abandoned recently. They're adapting, changing their methods. They know we're tracking them."

Emily's hand found his, her skin cooler than human but warmer than it had been months ago. Her dual nature had stabilized, giving her unprecedented control over both her human and vampiric aspects.

"We're making progress," she reminded him. "The Society reports supernatural activity down thirty percent from last month. The barriers are strengthening."

Seth nodded, sipping his tea. "I've been working on something new. A way to use my chronicler abilities not just defensively, but offensively. If I can write reality into being, maybe I can write these elder vampires out of—"

He froze mid-sentence, his eyes fixed on something in the street below. A tall figure stood motionless amid the swirling snow, face tilted upward toward their window. Even from this distance, Seth recognized the elegant posture, the perfectly tailored coat, the predatory stillness.

The mug slipped from Seth's fingers, shattering on the floor. Tea splashed across the hardwood, but he barely noticed.

Emily rushed to his side, alarmed by his sudden pallor. "Seth? What is it? What did you see?"

Seth's throat constricted, the name catching like a bone. "It's him."

"Who?" Emily pressed, peering into the snowy darkness.

Seth gripped the windowsill, knuckles white with tension. "That bastard the vampire. He's back!"

Epilogue
Future Landscapes

Seth stood beneath the cherry blossoms of Tokyo University's central quad, watching petals drift across the path where Hana Tanaka sat sketching in her notebook. The young novelist's pen moved with fluid grace, unaware that her recent dreams of creatures with too-sharp teeth and ancient hunger had begun manifesting in the real world. Small things at first: shadows that moved against the light, whispers in empty rooms, a strange man watching her from across crowded streets.

"She's the seventh this year," Emily murmured beside him, her eyes tracking the subtle shimmer of creative energy surrounding the young woman. "They're getting younger."

Seth nodded. "Sebastian always preferred established writers with something to lose. The other elders seem less discriminating."

They'd developed a system over the past year to identify potential chroniclers before the vampires could. They would approach them carefully then offer them protection and training. Some joined the Society; others simply accepted wards and warnings, choosing to remain in their normal lives with enhanced awareness. Either way, each new chronicler they saved was one less weapon the interdimensional vampires could use.

"Faith's report came in," Emily said, checking her phone. "The Berlin team intercepted another recruitment attempt. Writer was already being groomed by one of Sebastian's old network."

"Did they get a name?" Seth asked, his attention still fixed on Hana.

"No, but the vampire's methods matched what we know of the Prague coven."

Seth's jaw tightened. The Prague coven had been Sebastian's closest allies, the first to reorganize after his defeat. They'd adapted quickly, learning from his mistakes, becoming more subtle in their approaches to potential chroniclers.

"We should move soon," Seth said. "Before she starts writing the dreams down in detail."

The moment a potential chronicler began documenting supernatural encounters, they created a connection. It worked like a beacon drawing vampiric attention. Hana's dreams were already dangerous; her fiction could become deadly.

His phone vibrated with a message from Higgins: *Monthly council meeting tomorrow. Your presence requested. Bring the latest survey entries.*

The Society had transformed under Higgins' leadership. After purging corrupted elements, a painful process that had cost lives and trust, they'd established new protocols for dealing with supernatural threats. The old hierarchies had been flattened, field agents given more autonomy, knowledge shared more freely.

Connie now headed a specialized division tracking resurrection rituals worldwide. Three attempts had been thwarted in the past year, though at significant cost. The last one, in Cairo, had claimed two agents' lives.

Seth touched the leather-bound journal in his coat pocket. His abilities had become much more refined through practice and necessity. He could now bind, banish, or reveal supernatural entities with carefully chosen words, though he used this power sparingly. The corrupting potential of such abilities wasn't lost on him.

"She's leaving," Emily said, straightening as Hana packed her sketchbook and stood.

They followed at a discreet distance, watching for signs of surveillance. Faith's fieldwork had proven invaluable in developing these techniques, her transformed abilities allowing her to perceive threats across multiple planes of reality. Combined with Emily's unique vampire-human perspective, they gathered vital information about the Unknown that Seth then chronicled.

Together, the three had begun writing "The Rose and Raven Vampire Surveys," a comprehensive guide documenting vampire bloodlines, abilities, weaknesses, and methods of combat. Each entry was imbued with subtle power that weakened the vampires it described, a weaponized encyclopedia that grew more potent with each addition.

The First Book remained their greatest asset, kept in a hidden vault beneath the rebuilt Society headquarters under constant surveillance. Occasionally, it shifted and stirred, rewriting passages on its own as the supernatural world changed around them. Seth had learned to interpret these changes, to understand the book's warnings and revelations.

As they approached Hana's apartment building, Seth felt a familiar pressure again building behind his eyes, but it was not painful anymore. A vision began to form.

"Seth?" Emily touched his arm, recognizing the signs.

"I'm fine," he assured her, blinking to clear his sight. "Just a flash."

But the image lingered. It was an ancient figure watching from shadows, seven empty writing desks arranged before it. Mortus, denied his resurrection through Sebastian, but patient, always patient.

"Let's make contact tomorrow," Seth said, refocusing on their immediate task. "After she finishes her morning class."

Emily nodded, her eyes scanning the darkening street. "Another chronicler to protect."

"Another ally in the war," Seth corrected, his hand resting on his journal. The chronicles of this conflict had only just begun, but for the first time since Cornwall, he felt they might actually stand a chance.

About the Author
Beckett Blaise

Life is indeed stranger than fiction, which is why Beckett Blaise has such a strong sense of humor. Many of the off the wall things that happen to his protagonists have actually happened to him in real life! The more outlandish and unbelievable the thing, the more likely it actually happened. When he decided to write books, he made only one rule: I will not hold back and will just let myself go no matter how offensive or dirty the dish! I don't want to worry about anything. I just want to tell the story my way. That's his mantra, credo, and promise and he lives by it.

Beckett hails from Texas but he never felt he fit in to the Texas crowd. He has always been different and that's all right with him. He loves Science Fiction, Fantasy, and Horror. Sometimes he likes all three at once. He writes to be free, so he writes freely. Fantasy means you fantasize about things real and unreal, so if you can dream up things like demons, aliens, vampires, wizards, and more you can fit them into any story.

www.ingramcontent.com/pod-product-compliance
Lightning Source LLC
LaVergne TN
LVHW041659060526
838201LV00043B/495